Gardens of the God

A NOVEL BY

BILL GETZ

THE REDWOOD PRESS
California
2012

Published by
The Redwood Press
4107 Constitution Avenue
Fairfield, CA 94533

© 2012 by Bill Getz
All rights reserved. No part of this book may be reproduced or transmitted in any form or by any means, electronic or mechanical, including photocopying, recording, or by any information storage and retrieval system, without permission in writing from the copyright owner.

This is a work of fiction. Any similarity between characters and places in this story and real persons and places is coincidental.

First paperback edition, The Redwood Press, 2012

ISBN 13: 0-941196-07-0

AUTHOR'S COMMENTS

After reading this story, you may come to the conclusion that this fiction presents a more rational reality than what we have long been led to believe. A challenge.

The author owes a debt of gratitude to his wife, Vicki, who has had to put up with this writing nonsense, and did her usual masterful job of editing errors out of the manuscript. The book would never had been completed without her.

Daughter Linda Murphy, good friends, Gil Ferrey, and James Lynch, M.D., were additional "volunteer" editors to whom I owe my gratitude. Nevertheless, the author is responsible for all errors they missed.

Dedicated to Jo and Dr. Ray. On another plain, at another time, but not forgotten.

Bill Getz

Prologue

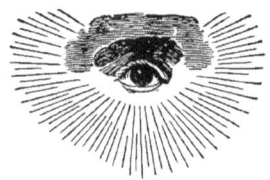

I am a teller of tales - tales of love and hate, ancient times and new, war and peace, life and death. *This is a story about death.*

I know, I know, you say, *What a macabre subject. How gruesome. Why would you have me read about such an unhappy event? It is arrogance to believe that I would waste my time on a subject I prefer to forget.*

Aha, I say, your mind is of Stygian set, influenced by the ancients' philosophy who have made death a bawdry word by writing such dribble as . . .

> *Who is this ghoul who fills the night*
> *With visions of horror and screams of fright?*
> *Who is this hooded ghost whose goal*
> *To wield a scythe and harvest the soul?*

Alas, these ancients were wrong. Those men of yore made mockery of mankind's greatest triumph of life - it is death.

This, my friend, is not a story of death as the familiar, fearful, final phenomenon, nor death as an unknown beginning, but death as a primal part of the cyclical thread of life. It is a story of hope. It is a story of promise, one that says that human life has a purpose that is neither mystical, nor transient, nor trivial.

The story is not a Greek tragedy, but an American triumph. There are only two experiences shared by all humanity past, present and future, and they are *life and death*. You know life, it is fleeting. But what do you know about death? Little, I suspect, *yet it is eterna*l.

When the tale is done, you may or may not be pleased by my story, but you will at least be the wiser for the effort.

In the year of our Lord, Nineteen Hundred Eighty-six . . . .

Chapter 1

Frank A. Picariello is well qualified to speak about death. He is an Anesthesiologist and Professor of Medicine at a prestigious university. Dr. Picariello and Death are daily companions, sometimes competitors, sometimes colleagues, sometimes friends, sometimes foes. At this moment they are foes, locked in a struggle of such monumental dimensions that the outcome will eternally determine whether the doctor's black-hooded adversary will be forever banished into the realms of mythology, or will continue to sting the human race. In less than an hour the battle will be drawn. Defeat or victory will be known, and the world may never again be quite the same.

As he sat in the staff lounge contemplating the three curses of the profession, *waiting, worrying, wondering* what is to come, Frank Picariello recalled that it was here that it all began. *Can it be just seven months ago*, he mused. It seems like an eternity, an appropriate thought. After all, he is a member of a medical team in search of eternity . . . .

. . . . and they may have found it.

* * * * * *

Seven Months Earlier

The appendectomy had been routine. Dr. Picariello had started with an IV of sodium pentathol, and the ten-year old patient would be out of bed by the next day. Healthy ten-year olds are a marvel of mending. The surgeon, Bob Dickson, did his usual competent job. Afterwards, Frank had an hour before he was due back into surgery, a hysterectomy. Those operations are emotional as well as physical traumas. *Probably use a spinal,* he thought to himself as he sipped his coffee.

He was on his second cup that memorable day when Joe came into the lounge. Joe is Joseph Raymond Cleary, M.D., a cardiovascular surgeon, and like Frank, a Professor of Medicine. Both are on the faculty of the University's Medical School. Doctors Frank and Joe had been close friends since they were kids.

Joe Cleary was also in his pale green scrubs, shirt and pants, face mask dangling loosely around his neck. His abundant brown hair, sprinkled with grey at the temples, was partly hidden by the standard disposable green paper cap.

Frank knew instantly that something was on Joe's mind. The usual good-natured sparkle in Joe's eyes was replaced by a detached look that suggested his thoughts were elsewhere.

Eyes are what Frank notices first. He sees only the eyes in the operating rooms, above the masks. He had become adept at reading the signals, the messages that constantly flash like two TV screens to the mind. Danger, indecision, puzzlement, contemplation, victory, disappointment, danger - it's all there, in the eyes.

Joe's large, brown eyes were expressive even while his face remained disciplined, expressionless. A learned trait important to those who make daily, instant life and death decisions. More often than not, Joe's eyes were full of his Irish grandfather's twinkle. This morning, however, his face was not broken into the restrained wrinkles by his usual tightlipped smile, and his eyes suggested more of his German than his Irish lineage. Then he saw Frank Picariello and walked over to the table.

"Morning, Frank, how's the Chief Gasser this fine day?" His standard greeting lacked enthusiasm.

"Hi, Joe. Chipper, thanks, and how about the Chief Butcher?" the standard response. "What's new?" Frank knew that Joe had something on his mind, and Frank was his standard sounding board. It had been the same since their grade school days.

Joe set his cup on the table and his lean, five-feet eleven frame onto a chair. The two were both the same age, 41, but Joe remained slim while Frank was well down the pot road. That's fat at the waist, not something you smoke. Too much of Frank's Italian mother's pasta and biscotti cookies.

Joe was quiet for a moment, studying the rising steam from his coffee. Around the lounge, doctors in surgical garb or white coats or business suits, were talking or watching TV, drinking liquids they tell their patients to forebear, munching sweet rolls loaded with sugar and fat, testament to the hypocrisy also found among Hippocratic practitioners.

Joe took several sips of the dark brown liquid, guaranteed to raise the pulse and maybe even the cholesterol levels, and then started talking with a subdued intensity in his voice that Frank recognized from many years of association. Joe was intentionally controlling his enthusiasm to maintain that inscrutable dignity that students expect of a Professor of Medicine. Finally, Joe allowed his thoughts to give birth to words.

"Frank, do you remember that female patient by the name of Sims that we operated on together about a year ago? In her middle fifties. Had a mitral insufficiency. We gave her a pig valve. Remember? We lost her for about three minutes. She had an absolute flat," referring to her brain trace as registered on an electroencephalograph, or EEG for short.

"But we brought her back. The next day she told us about watching us operate on her, and hearing our conversation. Really incredible stuff."

"Sure, I remember," Frank responded. "She was one excited lady. Talked about traveling down some tunnel with a bright light at the end, and seeing her dead parents, that sort of thing. I've been around five or six similar cases, but Sims seemed to have had the most vivid recollection of any of them. So, what about her?"

"That's the one, and let me tell you old friend, I've had a few other patients that had similar experiences, but nothing like the Sims case. I didn't mention it to you before, but I kept in touch with her for several months, even though she was from Phoenix.

"That operation did more than change her heart valve. Her whole life took on a new meaning as she described it, and she seemed very genuine. She told me some amazing stories."

"Like what?" Frank interjected knowing that Joe would tell him anyway. Frank was always good at playing second fiddle to Joe.

"Well, for one thing," Joe said, "she told me about the operation in more detail than she had at first. Said she was afraid that we might laugh at her. Do you know, Frank, that even with the anesthetic screen over her head, she described details of the surgery that would have been impossible for her to observe unless she was either looking over my shoulder, or looking from above as she claims.

"She saw us cut into her chest, use the electric saw on the sternum, she saw the whole procedure. She even commented about the size and shape of her heart, noting that one part of it was a different color caused by the heart attack. Now, how in the hell could a patient describe *that* about their own operation?"

"That's not entirely unusual, Joe" Frank said. "I have had patients tell me what the surgical team was chatting about during surgery, but only if I had used paralytic agents with the anesthesia. They did not, however, have any out-of-body experience like you are talking about."

"True enough." Joe said, "She could have subconsciously heard the conversation, but how would my patient also be able to report what the team was wearing? She mentioned seeing blood stains on my green shoe covers. I don't know, Frank, but it was convincing evidence the lady was an observer as well as a patient. Spooky."

"*Spooky* is a good word for it," Frank replied.

Joe continued. "Then again, what she told me about her life after the operation is really what piqued my interest to look into this phenomenon. Besides what might be expected - no longer fearing death - she had an almost religious outlook concerning the meaning of life and the nature of reality. Mrs. Sims said she had discovered a new knowledge not possessed before.

"I pressed her about this, and she said she could not pin it down, but in everyday conversation, or reading, or watching TV, she often understood technicalities about subjects that she had absolutely no previous knowledge."

"Are you telling me, Joe, that the Sims woman believes she is smarter since her near-death experience" That she knows things she did not know before? That's a real stretch!" Frank expressed.

"That is not only what she says", Joe quickly replied, "but that is what her husband and adult son also say. They are baffled."

"Come on, Joe, that sounds like so much malarkey to me. How can you prove anything like that?"

"I know, this borders on the supernatural, and it sounds like nonsense, but Mrs. Sims is different. She isn't trying to sell anything. Truthfully, it was difficult for me to get information out of her *because* she is aware of how far-fetched her story sounds.

"Just the same, Frank, it was my exposure to Sims that got me started looking into these so-called near-death experiences. They apparently are common enough that they are now referred to as *NDEs*.

"I've done some reading on the subject, the usual stuff like Meyer's *Human Personality and Its Survival of Bodily Deaths*, as well as books by Kubler-Ross, Moody, Ring, to name a few published over a decade ago. Even the medical journals have gotten into the act. There have been a few good articles in the *Journal of Psychiatry*. You may be surprised how many journals have reported on these so-called NDEs over the years.

"When I first read about this stuff in medical journals, I passed it off as fringe medicine, even though Swiss born Kubler-Ross is an M.D., as are some of the other authors. I didn't get too excited because most of the cases were just reports of what patients thought they encountered, mostly on operating tables, but some in non-medical environments like automobile accidents, drowning victims, even in their own beds.

"Before you say it, Frank, I know that anecdotal reports do not make sound scientific proof of anything. Scientific truths are not established by testimonials, opinions, surveys or questionnaires."

Frank finally got a word in. "I don't think I know where this is heading, Joe? Should I?"

Joe smiled. "Be patient with your elderly friends" - Joe was five months older than Frank - "but I had another NDE patient yesterday that even tops the Sims case. It has caused me to reconsider my initial reactions about these near death experiences."

"What happened?" Frank asked, drawing him deeper into the subject. "Whatever it was has sure made a change in you, that's a fact."

"For a reason," Joe said. "We were in the middle of a triple bypass when we lost the patient. His brain wave went flat. Of course he was on the pump, but absolutely no stimulant response for about five minutes. We were worried about permanent brain damage, but getting him back was the priority. We got him back, and since we had already completed the bypass, we patched him up, started his heart, and cleaned up without further complications.

"Then this morning I stopped by the ICU to see how he was doing. He was awake and bright. Everything appeared normal, but this male, age fifty-eight, was obviously bursting to tell someone his experiences during surgery.

"I let him talk and I took notes. He had an episode that sounded much like the Sims story. He said the last thing he remembered before the anesthetic knocked him out was the fuzzy outline of doctors and nurses looking down on him, talking to him through masked faces just before the anesthesia shield was put in place. Then everything went black, and in an instant - he said he had no sense of time - he went from the black void to a state of clear, sharp, bright reality. He found himself looking down from directly above the operating table.

"He said that his first thought was, 'What in the hell am I doing up here?' On second thought he said he believed he was supposed to be up there. Nothing unusual.

"He described the whole procedure that was taking place below him, and like Sims, he even mentioned what we were saying. Maybe his anesthetized brain could hear what we said, or maybe, as you suggested, Frank, he had a paralytic drug in his anesthetic, but whatever the cause, there was no way he could see us with the anesthesia screen over his head.

"Then the patient said that he moved to the corner of the room, above everything, and continued to watch until I had said, 'Close him up.' This was the point where we lost him."

Frank interrupted. "Up to that point there was no indication of anything wrong?"

"Nothing," Joe replied. "Everything had been normal, and just like the Sims case, this patient said he felt himself being propelled at lightning speed through a tunnel, although he called it a 'passage of energy.' He described a sun-like light at the end of the tunnel, and as he got closer he was overwhelmed with a feeling of peace, warmth and love, so intense he could find no human words to describe it.

"He went on to say that he also started to feel a strong urge to return to his body, but he didn't really want to go back. He said it was if there was a voice or a presence telling him that it wasn't his time, and he still had an important role to play in life. His next recollection was finding himself in bed in the ICU unit."

"An interesting story for sure, Joe, but not unlike those we have heard before," Frank volunteered, not too helpfully.

"True, Frank, but I haven't finished the story, and here is where it gets real interesting. I had many questions to ask him, but the ICU nurse kept giving me an icy stare and I knew I had overstayed my welcome. I did get one statement from him that encouraged me to want to talk to him again. Here, let me read his exact words," and Joe pulled a notebook from his pocket. *While I was close to the light, I knew that I was in communication with total intelligence. I could think of any question on any subject and I would instantly know the answer.*

"You already know, Frank, that I am hyped about this latest case, but even before this and the Sims case, I had been toying with an idea, and I wanted to get your reaction."

Aha, Frank thought, *here it comes.* He knew that Joe was too conservative to get enthusiastic about every idea that popped into his head, and he was obviously fired up about this new one. Frank did have one concern in the back of his mind. It crept in on cautious feet when Joe started talking about the Sims case.

Joe had had a very tragic experience three years ago. He lost his wife Linda and their six-year old daughter, Becky, in an automobile accident. A drunk driver hit them. This tore Joe apart. He developed a terrible sense of guilt, believing the accident would never had happened if he had been driving as he was originally supposed to do. A medical emergency demanded his attention, and he had to cancel his plan to take Linda and Becky to a first grade party. Joe and Linda were close, high school sweethearts and all that implies.

Joe's life revolved around Becky, a dark-haired beauty who was a miniature of her mother. It had only been in the past six months that Joe began to shed some of the heavy cloak of grief, and enter what is sometimes euphemistically called a state of normalcy. However, this sort of trauma burns a brand of loss on the heart. The question that came to Frank's mind because of Joe's new interest, *Is Joe slipping back, obsessed with death?*

"Frank, my colleague and friend . . ."

Here it comes, Frank thought as Joe continued.

"Do you realize the medical profession has never made a serious attempt to study death?"

"Well, to be perfectly honest, Joe, I've never thought anything about it myself other than what we see almost every day in the hospital. Death seems like a good thing to avoid."

Joe's statement was confirming Frank's fears that he was not over his deep grief. Frank asked, reluctant to hear the answer, "Just why would anyone want to study death other than being certain a person is dead? I realize it was not too long ago that we considered a person dead when their heart stopped, and no serious attempts were made to resuscitate the patient. That has all changed, so what are you thinking, Joe?"

"I am thinking that like any scientific problem, death should be the subject of a scientific research project."

"Death?" Frank questioned. "Do you mean a study of the so-called *near death experiences*? If so, I should think that has been studied to death, if you will excuse the pun. As we said earlier, there are all kinds of books and articles on the subject. It is hardly a new subject. What possible additional research could you do?" Now Frank was becoming really concerned for Joe.

Frank continued, "There was a movie quite a few years ago about some medical students who were experimenting with putting each other to death and then being resuscitated, kind of like a game or something. I believed it was named *Flatliner* or *Flatline*. Never made big time."

Joe had an amused smile on his face as he recognized the worry in Frank's voice. In many ways, Joe and Frank had been like brothers since they were young, always taking care of each other when the occasion arose.

"No, I never heard of the movie," Joe responded. "I'll admit that what I am saying may seem goofy, but then many ideas probably sounded strange at first, like Michelangelo making drawings for an airplane. No, I am not suggesting we go down that NDE road again, although the information would be helpful.

"No, what I had in mind is to study the death state itself. Think about it. If we can resuscitate a patient after they have been brain dead, have you ever asked the questions, were they dead in the first place, and if so, exactly where were they, and what does *they* mean, the mind, the soul, or what?

"All we have now about the death state is from religion or from NDE people. Religions depend upon faith, NDEs upon what they perceive as reality, neither of these groups are a basis for scientific proof of anything. We know that death is a process, not an instant in time, or at least I think we agree to that. That raises another question, at what point does the death state become irreversible?

"The bottom line is, Frank, death is an unknown, and the unknown is the scientist's greatest challenge. It is also his only reason to exist as a scientist.

"I remember reading Medawar's book a few years ago, you know the one, *The Limits of Science*. I was impressed with his story about the derivation of the Spanish royal family coat-of-arms and how it applies to the ever-changing field of medicine.

"According to Medawar, before Columbus made his first voyage, the national motto of the Royal Family of Spain- was *Non Plus Ultra, there is no beyond*, a reference to the fact that Spain took pride in believing the Straits of Gibraltar, bounded by the so-called *Pillars of Hercules*, were the end of the earth. After Columbus returned and dispelled that notion, the Royal Family took the easy way out and eliminated the negative in the motto, and it now became, *Plus Ultra, there is a beyond*. If only medical research was that simple.

"Columbus had the faith of his convictions, and the guts to sail beyond the ends of the earth to prove them. That is what scientists and explorers have in common. Seeking the truth, exploring the unknown.

"It was in another book I read, I believe by Rhine of Duke University, a controversial parapsychologist. He said, *It is timely for the scientist to peer over the edge of his physical foundations and ask, What, if anything, may follow the final obliterating blast?* He's right, you know. It is time."

Frank had patiently and apprehensively listened to Joe as he seriously exposed his thoughts. Frank had to ask, and he did so with great trepidation, "Joe, do I understand correctly, are you about to suggest there should be a University sponsored project to research death?"

Joe replied with a mischievous look in his Irish eyes, "I always knew you were a bright boy, Frank, for a *Dago*." He continued with a deadpan face, "That is exactly what I mean!"

Chapter 2

Joseph Raymond Cleary, M.D. had to cut short his conversation with Frank A. Picariello, M.D., because of his surgery schedule. He could tell from Frank's reaction to his research proposal that he was quite skeptical. *Can't say that I blame him* was Joe's thought. Joe believed that anyone who has not had the opportunity to do the homework, to really study the subject, that the idea of researching the death state must seem like some sort of science fiction, or off-the-wall pseudo science, maybe as weird as that movie Frank had mentioned. Skepticism, however, was not a deterrent to Dr. Joe.

Joe could read Frank well enough after all these years to believe Joe was being influenced by the loss of his wife and daughter. Joe admitted to Frank that their death had an overwhelming effect upon his life, and perhaps, had heightened his interest in the subject of death. Joe honestly believed, and had told Frank, that no medical doctor worth his degree can be immune to death. No doctor likes to lose a patient. It is like a personal failure. Sometimes it is, and that makes it worse. Joe was a very humane medic. Losing family is different.

Joe assured Frank that the loss of Linda and Becky was not the motivation for the research, but the doubt hung in Frank's mind.

* * * * * *

For the next month Joe only saw Frank in passing in the halls of the hospital. It was a busy month. Their schedules did not put them together in surgery.

Then one evening Frank telephoned Joe at home. He said that he and his wife Angel - her real name is Angelina, but her Italian mother and father gave her the nickname - had just finished a late dinner, part of the penalty of the profession. He said their three kids were now either doing homework or watching television. Angel was still cleaning up the dinner dishes.

Frank said he had just finished reading an article in the latest issue of *Anesthesiology*, journal of the American Society of Anesthesiologists, and it was on the subject of handling patients who have had to be resuscitated. It made him think of their earlier conversations about research on death, so without coming straight out and saying so, Frank was curious as to where Joe stood on the project. In his backhanded manner, Frank finally got to the point of his call.

"Are you busy, Joe? Angel thought you might enjoy a cup of coffee and her biscotti cookies, freshly baked. Why don't you drop over? We haven't seen you for several weeks."

Joe knew immediately that Frank wanted to talk about the research project. Joe always believed that Italians were oblique about many things. Never directly to the point because they think it rude. He did not consider himself an expert on Italians, being Irish and having been married to an Irish lass, but when he and Frank were boys, the Irish and the Italians lived in adjoining neighborhoods, and Frank's home was a second home to Joe. He sometimes felt closer to Frank's mom and dad than he did to his own. Joe's dad was the stereotyped Irishman, drank too much, and he was a cop. He treated his wife very badly, and wasn't much better to Joe or his sister Patricia. Joe ate many meals cooked by Frank's mother. So he told Frank on the phone, "Fine, I'll be right over." It took him ten minutes.

Frank lived in a ranch style, shake roof house, built on two acres among large Live and Coastal Oaks, eucalyptus, pine and elm trees, just down the street from Joe. Their street was part of a development begun fifteen years earlier by a medical doctor, Ralph Anderson. He owned thirty acres in these lush, wooded foothills, and sold off two-acre parcels to medical doctors and dentists. The locals called it, *Pill Hill*. It is only a fifteen minute drive to the University Hospital and Medical School where Frank and Joe were on the faculty.

After Linda and Becky were lost, Joe lived alone. That had not helped his recovery from grief, with all the constant reminders around the house, and the fact that he still kept Becky's room just as it was on the day she died. Joe was aware that Frank and Angel believed this a little maudlin, and had been after Joe to redecorate the whole house. Joe had decided that he would do that soon. The house needed updating.

Vicki Wentworth is another one encouraging Joe. She is a surgical nurse and had dated Joe a couple times in the past few months. A very lovely young lady, but Joe believed he just did not have the time nor energy to devote to the house, or to Vicki.

Joe still remembered the day he met Frank Anthony Picariello. It was a bright sunny day in early September, the first day of school at Saints Peter and Paul Grade School. Both of them were entering sixth grade. Frank was the new kid, his family had just moved into the city from a small valley town about sixty miles away. His dad had bought into a wholesale vegetable and fruit market owned by Frank's great uncle, his grandfather Picariello's brother.

Frank's father, Mario Picariello, had farmed for twenty years on his father's farm, but now he wanted to get his own business. His two brothers were still on the farm and could help their dad.

It was a big decision for Frank's dad and mom to move away from the family and start over in strange surroundings. Frank's great uncle, Sebastiano, who everyone called "Charlie," and his wife, Lena, welcomed the family with open arms, mother and father, Frank and his two brothers, one older, one younger than Frank, and two younger sisters.

Frank was a skinny, shy farmer kid, dressed like a country bumpkin that he was, when he arrived at Sister Jane de Chantel's sixth grade classroom, devoid of friends and scared of this new, strange world.

At recess, twelve-year old Joe went up to Frank and said, "Hi, I'm Joe Cleary, and I would like to be your friend." That made all the difference in the world to the poor Italian boy from the "sticks," and they became friends for life from that moment.

* * * * * *

After Joe and Frank were settled in the den with a cup of expresso and Angel's cookies, and some small talk about Frank's recent attack of gout, Frank finally got around to the question he had been eager to ask. As a Teller of Tales, I was going to say, *dying to ask*, but that seemed a little trivial. Frank tried to make his question sound as if he just thought of it.

"By the way, Joe, have you given any more thought to your research idea about death?"

Joe expected the question and promptly said, "I have not only been thinking about it, I even drafted a proposal," and as he was saying this, pulled a stapled group of papers from his briefcase. "This is a draft copy for you, Frank. I want you to be co-director."

Joe didn't want his friend to start asking questions yet, or to start reading the paper, so he kept on talking. All Frank had time to do was to note the title on the paper, *Proposal for a Study of the Death Phenomenon.*

"You and I, Frank," Joe continued, "and all the rest of humanity live in two worlds. One is the world of physical reality, the flesh and bones, and all that we can see, touch, smell and occupy. The other world is a quiet one, a subdued and very private world of the mind, where thoughts and dreams and mental images are not shared, but remain the exclusive property of each individual. It is in this second world where judgments are made, sensual sensations created, reasoning formed, our movements directed, all of which makes each one of us a distinct personality. You and I, Frank, we deal with the first world of flesh and bones. Rosie Willett deals with the second world of the mind."

"Aha," Frank jumped in, "so you talked Rosie into the deal."

I better explain "Rosie" that Frank and Joe mentioned. She is a real character around the Medical School, but then I, with my Teller of Tales bias, have never met a psychiatrist that I didn't think was a little strange, a private prejudice.

Rosie is also a real *doll*. Of course no one called her "Rosie" to her face when she first joined the faculty. The rumor had spread that would result in a severe and cutting rebuke from her. She was *Doctor* Rosamond Willett, M.D., PhD, a Psychiatrist, and an Assistant Professor of Medicine. A few years later, Joe had inadvertently called her *Rosie* one day when she was observing a surgery Joe was performing. He apologized immediately and Rosie shot back with a startling reply.

"Hell, Joe, I got over that pomposity the first time an upperclassman in med school stuck a tube in the penis of my first cadaver to give it an erection. The guys had quite a laugh when I opened the lid and saw it. I just stared in horror and embarrassment for a few seconds at the poised phallus. Then I realized how funny it was, and despite my reputation to the contrary, became *one of the boys*. Call me Rosie anytime."

Rosie is a brassy, outspoken, *women's libber,* and one hell-of-a fine teacher. Now a full tenured professor, students love and fear her at the same time, the faculty amused, sometimes embarrassed by her antics, and the Administration always on edge waiting for her next outburst, which was frequent. Joe went on with his explanation of the project to Frank.

"The mind, dear friend, the mind. What is it, really? The soul of the human race? When the body dies, does the mind die with it? If it doesn't die, where does it go? A surgeon cuts into the brain but sees no thoughts, no mind. I cut into a heart and see no life, no spirit, no soul. Where are they? What are they? How much does a thought weigh? We know they exist, or at least something exists that we cannot see, but we give them names. What is the weight and dimensions of a thought? We cannot see them, but they are powerful forces that have changed our physical and nonphysical lives.

"The other day I was browsing through some of the old books in my library, and I came across one of Ambrose Bierce's books, I don't remember which one, perhaps his *The Devil's Dictionary,* and that triggered a memory of a passage, and I looked it up and jotted it down."

Joe pulled a small notebook from his briefcase and read from it. *The mind is a mysterious form of matter secreted by the brain. Its chief activity consists in the endeavor to ascertain its own nature, the futility of the attempt being due to the fact that it has nothing but itself to know itself with.*

"I thought that was a reasonable description of our ignorance about the mind. It is our paradox, Frank. We don't understand the mind, but it is our mind that must discover itself. I'm afraid to tell that to Rosie as she may raise the roof off the Med building."

"Look, Joe, you are getting into subjects and an area way beyond cardiovascular surgery. Why do you want to venture there?"

"Simple, old friend. Over the centuries there have been thousands of philosophical explanations and hypotheses that supposedly answer my questions, just as there are thousands of theological beliefs that have spawned from these questions. Many theologians are diametrically opposed to each other's beliefs. Who has the right answers? Who is wrong? Haven't you asked yourself those questions? Are you prohibited to think of matters not connected to anesthesiology?"

"I'll consider those rhetorical questions, Joe, but you are starting to scare me, but go on, I'm listening."

"Stay with me, Buddy. You'll see where I'm heading. Consider that we know we can kill the body, but do we also kill the psyche as well? If not, can we turn that knowledge into practical medical use? If the mind, the psyche, has a separate existence from the brain, that fact alone could change the practice of medicine. We cannot state that as a fact, of course, but as long as the possibility exists, we, as scientists, must pursue it. That is what I want to do, Frank. Those are the questions for which I want to seek answers."

Joe could read skepticism in Frank's eyes and facial expression. He was primed for his questions.

"Seems to me, Joe, you are raising questions best left to the theologians or to Rosie the Shrink. Why are we interested in the supernatural? We are mechanics, Joe, not philosophers. We're interested in fixing broken bones and diseased parts. Let the churches takes care of the sick souls, and Rosie take care of the sick minds."

"Frank, your argument has been used for centuries, maybe since the beginning of Homo sapiens. If we don't understand a question about the nature of man and the world around us, assign it to a deity. That relieves the ordinary man from having to think about it too much. It is a cop out. Every truth in science comes only after someone has imagined what the truth might be."

Frank's intellectual self was finally aroused as he jumped into the subject saying, "Some truths are discovered by chance, Joe, you know that, or as one of our colleagues said, *by happy guesses, felicitous strokes of inventive talent.*"

"That may be true," Joe replied, "but it is hardly the premise for serious scientific investigation. We may discover truth by chance, but we must establish the conditions that will give chance the opportunity to happen, wouldn't you agree?"

Joe didn't give Frank an opportunity to reply but continued. "The arrogance of man has always been the belief that humans are unlike all other life forms on the planet, and thus not subject to the same laws of nature.

"Nature theorists believe for the most part that the birds and the beasts, insects, flower and fauna, everything that lives, - except the human race - are subject to laws of nature and follow a pattern of nature, a cycle if you will. The same people say that all life, except man, has a purpose to nourish another part of nature, the so-called *food chain theory*. They assign the purpose of man is to *lord* over all this natural domain and to be served by it. That is not a purpose. It is a pompous excuse."

"You sound like you are back in the classroom giving one of your lectures, Joe. Where are you heading?" Frank asked.

At least Joe had Frank asking questions, so he knew he had to give him an answer to the point. "I agree that I have sounded a little like one of my classroom lectures, but after all, I am a teacher!

"The bottom line is that none of these pseudo scientists has ever considered the possibility that humans are as much a part of the cycle of nature as any other living creature. This is not a new idea. In the latter part of the Nineteenth Century, a German scholar proposed the same idea. I believe his name was von Haeckel. He concluded that man was a part of the natural world, a position supporting Darwin. They did not have the technology to pursue this beyond hypothesis and speculation.

"If that is true, my friend, then it means that humans have a purpose other than just to *lord over nature*. If we knew that purpose, we could practice our healing arts with a knowledge that could change our whole approach to what we do, why we do it, and how we do it. The key to this knowledge is to know more about the death state. If we can get answers to that, we will revolutionize the practice of medicine."

From the expression on Frank's face, it was obvious he was not following Joe's thought stream, so Joe asked him if he had any questions.

"No questions, Joe, but not because I understand, but because you can think much faster than most mortals, and you sometimes lose patience with us lesser beings that do not keep up with you. I'm not certain that I understand enough to ask an intelligent question. I think I follow what you are saying, but I am not certain where you're leading.

"Expecting the University to accept a study of death as an official research subject is a tall order. You know damn well how the medical faculty reacts to subjects involving metaphysics, telepathy, clairvoyance, extrasensory perception, and so forth. The faculty consider these subject as nonscientific, black magic kind of nonsense, impossible. These subjects are relegated to either the scientific wastebasket, or to second-rate schools. You must know, Joe, the faculty will place your proposed research into the same category, spooky science."

Frank was showing interest now as well as skepticism.

"The big question they are going to ask you, Joe, is just how does your proposal fit into medical research? What's the end benefit? That's what you and I are paid for, to find answers to problems that are going to help people, our patients. Seems to me our profession has received enough criticism for getting into social, legal and religious issues. Abortions come to mind, or the right-to-die issue. We ought to stick to what I said before, healing the sick."

Joe knew that if he couldn't persuade Frank to support his project, then he could not persuade anyone. Joe responded. "All right, let me try this on you. Stay with me for a few minutes and I'll relate my idea to the field of medicine.

"The psyche, the mind, is accepted as a part of a human. What do we know about it, say as compared to the anatomy?"

Joe answered his own question, "Damn little! Sure, there are tons of literature on the subject, but it all boils down to this. There are plenty of psychiatrists, psychologists and others in the transpersonal psychology fields, including theologians, who believe the mind consists of two distinct aspects, the active mind that controls bodily functions, and a subconscious that processes out subjective thoughts and our ability to analyze and visualize. A dualism of the mind is consistent with a dualism of the body and the mind, and the mind and the brain.

"We give many names to the mind. Socrates, Goethe and Jung called it the *psyche* as I have been calling it. Schopenhauer said it was the *will*. Freud had three names for it, *id, ego and the superego*. The Hindus call it *Manasa*, the higher mind, and the Church, of course, calls it the *soul*.

"Isn't it interesting, *Doctor* Frank, that biologically, the structure of the human body also has a dualism, a redundancy built into it? Two arms, two legs, two eyes and ears, two kidneys, two lungs, two sides of the brain, two sides to the heart. We call these *complementary dualism,* because the dual parts perform similar functions."

Frank piped in, "Thank God there is only one mouth, although some people speak out of both sides, and some speak with a *forked tongue*."

Joe smiled and let Frank have his little joke. Frank was trying to lighten the conversation, but Joe did not let him break his chain of thought.

"OK, wise guy, but continuing my lecture to the nonbeliever, the human also has an *opposite dualism* that is of equal importance. Perhaps they are merely extremes on the same scale rather than a dualism, but the same principle applies; light and darkness, sound and silence, pain and pleasure, hot and cold, wet and dry, physical and nonphysical, and, of course, life and death.

"As an Anesthesiologist, you *fool* the brain into believing there is no pain by drugging it. That is physical. Rosie Willett can *tell* the brain not to feel pain by hypnosis. That is nonphysical. You can explain scientifically why your gases and drugs work, but Rosie can only surmise why hypnosis works, and its been around longer than your drugs.

"Interesting facts that demonstrate our lack of knowledge of our nonphysical, but very real world, and critical to the practice of medicine."

Frank couldn't contain himself. His Italian blood was heating up. "Your *fooling the brain* comment seems to reduce my occupation to that of an educated con-artist, *and,* despite your apparent high regard for Rosie's hypnosis, I have never seen you use *her* during your surgeries. You still prefer my *gasses!"*

Laughing at his rise in temperament, Joe responded, "Not your self generated gasses, ole' Buddy. You do have a point. I'll concede that I prefer using the known to the unknown, but it is the latter to which I am addressing the project, the unknown."

"OK, Joe, you got my attention. I agree we know little about the mind, and little about how the brain operates for that matter, and almost nothing about death, but what does all of that have to do with you and me? You're a surgeon and I'm a brain *teaser"* . . . Frank was letting his feelings show through . . . "so, what is it you want to do?"

Joe noticed that Frank had not included himself into the scheme - yet.

"That is an easy question," Joe replied. *Mors est veritas suprema*, *Death is the ultimate moment of truth*. I want you, dear friend, to put me to death and then bring me back to life. It is that simple.

Chapter 3

Since their discussion in the staff lounge four weeks earlier, Frank had suspected that Joe wanted to be the subject of his own research. Hearing him say it now in Frank's own kitchen, confirmed his worst fears, not that Frank knew where Joe could find anyone else to volunteer for the role. Imagine the reaction to a question, "Excuse me, sir, would you please volunteer to die in the interests of science?" Frank supposed that Joe had thought of the same question.

"That's a clear statement, all right!" Frank responded. "As I understand it, all you want me to do is to murder my closest friend. Seems like a reasonable request. I mean, wouldn't anyone kill his best friend if they asked? What are friends for?" Frank couldn't hide the skepticism and sarcasm in his words. Besides his sarcastic comments, there was a little panic in his voice as he realized Joe was serious about this.

Joe took it well. He was probably expecting something like that from Frank. They knew each other like a book.

As he reached into his briefcase Joe said, "I hit you cold. Sorry, Frank. Just do a favor for me. Before you make up your mind about joining the project, and before we talk about it again, read my proposed protocol," - the fancy name they gave research proposals at the University - "and these," as Joe handed Frank some bound documents and five books.

A quick glance told Frank the documents were medical research reports and a ten-page bibliography. The books were

Emanuel Swendeborg's two books, *Heaven and Hell* and *The Other Side of Life*; *The Theory of Eternal Life* by Rodney Collins; *Life at Death* by Kenneth Ring; and *Recollections of Death: A Medical Investigation* by M. B. Sabom, M.D.

Frank had never heard of any of these books, nor read any of the papers, except he did remember Joe mentioning the name "Ring" during their earlier discussion.

Frank glanced at the titles of a few of the papers. The titles told him immediately they were written by academicians. It was the old adage, *Takes one to know one*. Consider this first paper as an example, titled, *Jung Parapsychology and the Near-Death Experience: Towards a Transpersonal Paradigm*. A mouthful of words meant to impress other academics. University professors have to produce this stuff to get peer recognition, promotions, and most important, tenure.

The title of the second paper was almost as bad: *The Centrality of Near-Death Experiences in Chinese Pure Land Buddhism*. The third one was more to the point, and probably one that Frank thought he would more likely read. It was titled, *Research into the Evidence of Man's Survival After Death*. Frank did not have time to look at the others, but Joe had made his point. He was certainly not alone in his interest into the phenomenon of death.

The two friends talked a little longer, but since they both had early morning surgery schedules, Joe went home around 11:00 PM.

The subject did not come up again with Joe until three weeks later. In the meantime, Frank read all the research papers and books Joe had lent him. Heady stuff! Frank went even further and picked up three more books from the library: *Science and the Evolution of Consciousness, The Phenomenon of Man,* and the *Tibetan Book of the Dead*.

The bibliography that Joe had given to Frank contained 271 titles of scholarly papers, articles and books on the subject of life and death and the hereafter, and many medical reports about near-death experiences. More heady stuff!

Frank was now ready to confess that after reading all this literature, mostly about death, there was a spark of interest developing in his researcher's mind. As Frank remarked before, researchers have an overdeveloped sense of curiosity for the unknown.

Then Frank read Joe's protocol, his proposal for the research project, and the spark lit a flame. He decided to accept Joe's invitation to be co-director of his project.

* * * * * *

At this point in the story, it would be helpful if you knew more about Dr. Joseph Cleary's background to understand what motivates him. Life is never simple.

Dr. Cleary's office was typical of the University environment, typical of a government environment. Sameness, drabness, austere, cold as the steel in the desk, with the only true personal touch the pictures of Joe's deceased wife and daughter, and his college degrees hanging on the wall.

Books and papers were stacked in disarray in and on the bookcase, the chairs and the shelves. Frank Picareillo enjoyed goading Joe about his office by saying it reminded him of his teenage daughters' bedrooms.

The only real distinctions between most offices at the University were their size and the names on the degrees and on the door, and the faces in the pictures. Joe clearly rated one of the larger offices as the Head of the Thoracic Surgery Division and a tenured, full Professor of Medicine. Even so, it wasn't much bigger than a walk-in closet.

Another advantage of position was that Joe shared a secretary with only one other staff member. Frank had to share his with three other doctors. At the moment, Frank was sitting in one of the two "guest" chairs in the office, the other one filled with papers and journals. Both doctors were wearing the standard uniform, a long white coat reserved for Professors of Medicine. Half-coats were worn by medical students, interns, residents and technicians. Both coats had the name of the university embroidered in red thread above the breast pocket, and a plastic name plate above the emblem.

Name plates were important. They identified the wearer's position in life at the University Medical School as either an M.D., student, technician, or nurse, and lately two newer specialties, Nurse Practitioner and Physician's Assistant.

Another identification device was the stethoscope. Most professors carried them in their coat's side pockets, their long coats being a sufficient status indicator.

The short coat staff usually wore the stethoscope around their necks with the ends dangling over their shoulders. This way no one could miss the fact you were a member of the *professional* medical staff. The standard joke was that the interns slept with them, and wore them in the shower. The nuances of position. As I, the Teller of Tales, poetically penned years ago, *Petty badges of pretentiousness prevalent in universities.*

Every research project at the School of Medicine that involved a human subject had to be approved by the aptly named *Human Subjects Committee* chaired by Joe's nemesis, Dr. Theodore Stanton of heart transplant fame. He was not quite as well-known as Barnard, DeBakey, Cooley or Shumway, much to Stanton's chagrin, but he was a power at the University. Around the Medical School he was called "The Great One," but that was *not* intended as a sign of respect.

Since the height of his fame, ten years ago, Stanton had grown into a jealous despot. He was now Dean of the Medical School.

Dr. Joe Cleary faced some obstacles, and they were not all related to the technicalities of his new proposed project.

Dr. Stanton also kept his position as Chair of Cardiovascular Surgery, a special department established just for him at the height of his fame. Under normal circumstances, the department would be combined with Thoracic Surgery under the Department of Surgery.

Dr. Joe Cleary, Division head of Thoracic Surgery, was under the Department of Surgery, and his reputation was growing. Sometimes, the line between thoracic and cardiovascular surgery was finer than a membrane. This irked Stanton who wanted no one to be as famous as he in the School of Medicine, and possibly upstaging his reputation, particularly someone not under his direct control. That is how he became Joe's nemesis, but this needs to be explained.

It started about ten years ago at the time Stanton was a rapidly rising star and was also Head of the then combined Thoracic and Cardiovascular Surgery Department. Joe was his Chief Resident. Joe already had his surgery boards, and was now a postgraduate fellow in the more specialized thoracic and cardiovascular surgery specialty under Stanton's tutelage

After three years, it was clear to the professional staff that Joe the student was as good as the teacher. Joe finished his residency and was made an Assistant Professor upon the recommendation of Dr. Stanton.

Most members of the medical professional faculty had a private practice to augment their meager University salaries, and to hone their technical skills. Some used their private practice for research.

The Great One discouraged what he called, "excessive private practice" by anyone in his organization. He didn't like the competition, and in his great arrogance, believed that working with him was compensation enough. Joe Cleary was the first member of the department to breach that unwritten law, although partly unwittingly. He had developed a thriving private practice because of his spreading reputation of technical excellence.

At first, Dr. Stanton's reaction was mild. He had a long talk with Joe about dedication to the job, loyalty and that nonsense that means nothing. For the most part, Joe ignored Stanton's advice. As Joe's reputation grew, together with his patient list, The Great One became more agitated.

One day there was the proverbial straw, but I'll have to digress a moment from my story about Joe and Frank's project so that it is clear why there were political problems, and yes, politics and personalities permeated the halls of science and academe as much as they do the halls of politicians and corporate board rooms.

Three years previously, Dr. Theodore Stanton had a fifty-year old female patient with mitral stenosis and aortic insufficiency. This condition is often caused by rheumatic fever in childhood, and was suspected in this patient. She also had scleroderma morphia, a rare disease where the connective tissues in and around the tiny blood vessels, the capillaries, become inflamed. As the inflammation heals, internal scarring often occurs. This makes the tissue shrink and become stiff, giving the skin a tight, shiny drum-like, dead looking appearance, hence the term *morphia* or *dead*. It was also possible the scleroderma attacked the heart valves of the patient.

This was the patient's second open-heart surgery. The first time was also performed by Ted Stanton with Joe Cleary as his Chief Resident, whose principle job during the surgery was to open and close the chest cavity. Stanton did only the heart work. As usual, Stanton had two operations in progress simultaneously, so they had to be closely timed. No room for anomalies.

On that first surgery, Joe had begun the opening procedure after the Anesthesiologist and the Cardiovascular Perfusionist, the guy that operated the heart-lung machine, also known as the *pump man*, had the patient's heart and lung functions being performed by the pump.

Due to one of those not infrequent unforeseen problems, Stanton was running behind schedule with the surgery in the adjoining operating room. Joe was forced to complete the operation on the fifty-year old female, which he was well-qualified to do.

It was clear the patient's mitral valve needed attention, and was the major source of the patient's problem. Because he was not the primary surgeon, Joe elected a *conservative* solution. Instead of replacing the valve, he merely did a mitral commissurotomy, which in this case was a removal of the hardened growth from around the heart valve. He did not believe there was enough damage to the valve to justify its replacement. The patient was out of bed the next day, although not out of the hospital, and she felt great. What galled the staff was that The Great One took credit for the surgery - and got his normal pay for doing it. Unfortunately, as it later turned out, Joe had not made the best medical decision for that patient.

Two years later, the same patient's condition had deteriorated again to where another operation was necessary, not an unusual situation when either rheumatic fever or the scleroderma is the underlying condition attacking the heart valves. By now, Stanton was the Chairman of his own Cardiovascular Surgery organization, which I mentioned earlier, and was personally accepting only a few private patients. He was making top University dollars.

However, because of the earlier operation, and because the female patient's physician was a close friend of Stanton's and chair of a committee to raise money for a University faculty chair to be named for Stanton, The Great One agreed to do the second operation and to do the actual surgery himself. He also promised the suspicious patient's husband that Stanton would be in the operating room from the time the patient was placed on the pump. The general public still believed The Great One was the best, although that was no longer the case.

Stanton's Chief Resident for the second operation was Dr. Walter *Wally* Deer. He was a fine technician and in his fourth year of residency. Like many interns and residents, Wally Deer had been worked too hard in the previous week and had lost three patients, including a child, through no fault of his own. This operation on the fifty-year old female would be the first time he performed a chest opening on a patient that had a previous opening.

Some of the interns and residents at the University Hospital, a teaching hospital, worked as many as 120 hours a week. It was a disgrace and dangerous. There should be a law against it like in New York. Too many patients die from fatigue, not theirs, but their surgeon's. Some of the older faculty members opposed limitations. They consider the long hours a necessary *rites of passage* for the new doctors and specialists. They never ask the patients for their opinion.

Wally Deer was scheduled to start the chest opening at 8:30 AM after the cardiopulmonary pump was attached and operating. He began thirty minutes early with the pump not yet fully primed, his first mistake.

The principal surgeon, Dr. Ted Stanton was again in a second operating room performing another surgery. Although he limited his number of surgeries, when they were scheduled, he preferred to do two in one round-robin session early in the morning.

In the room with Wally Deer, besides the Anesthesiologist, Dr. Benjamin Welch, and the Perfusionist, there were the *scrub nurse* and two *circulating nurses*. There was no Board Certified thoracic surgeon as scheduled and required by hospital protocols. A second mistake.

Either because of fatigue or his inexperience with second openings, Deer did not think about the possibility of the heart being attached to the sternum, the breast bone, by adhesions from the first operation, those fibrous growths that often accompany the healing process after surgery. In the case of this patient, there were adhesions, and the heart was attached to the sternum.

With the surgical equivalent of an electric buzz saw, Wally cut down the sternum and right through the right auricle and ventricle of the patient's heart. Panic broke loose as the patient's blood pumped into the chest cavity and her blood pressure dropped to almost zero. Wally Deer hit the panic button, an actual alarm signal that sounds in every operating room. The scrub nurse was the one who pushed the red button on the wall upon Wally's order. Any doctor that is free is supposed to respond immediately.

All is created and goes according to order, yet o'er our lifetime rules an uncertain fate, according to Johann von Göthe. Thus, it was fate that placed Dr. Joe Cleary, our Joe, in an adjoining surgical suite where he had just finished a right lung lobectomy. Joe was the first physician to respond to the panic call, which over the hospital's loud speaker system blared "Stat, Surgery 3."

In seconds, Joe's quick mind analyzed the situation, read the instruments and saw the confusion in Wally Deer's eyes. Joe acted quickly. He completed the opening of the chest cavity to expose the damaged heart. The heart was wildly pumping blood into the chest cavity. Joe ordered the nurse to suction off the blood as he picked up the throbbing, wounded heart. There was a two-inch incision where the electric disc saw had sliced. Joe called for an electric *Fibrillator* to begin the process of stopping the beating heart. He couldn't repair a throbbing heart.

After stopping the fibrillation, Joe put an *X-clamp* on the ascending aorta, and injected high potassium in that part of the aorta closest to the heart. The potassium finally stilled the wounded, pulsating organ.

Joe quickly cannulated the aorta and the *Vena cava*, which means he attached plastic tubes to the aorta and Venus arteries to isolate the heart from the circulatory system of the body. The tubes were attached to the heart-lung machine which took over the heart pumping function as well as the job of the lungs to oxygenate and clean the blood. Joe had the patient operating from the heart-lung machine within three minutes after entering the operating room. He had no idea this was the same patient he had operated on two years earlier.

Joe then began suturing the ruptured heart just as Dr. Theodore Stanton, The Great One, came bustling into the room. He took one minute to size up the situation, being briefed as Joe continued his calm but hasty repair of the wounded patient. Stanton then said, "OK Joe, I'll take it from here," and with that he practically pushed Joe out of the way.

Dr. Stanton should have just closed the patient's cavity and tried again some other time to repair the diseased valves after the patient regained strength, if ever. As it was, she was without adequate blood pressure for five minutes or more, enough time for the brain to lose significant oxygen with all the possibilities of permanent brain damage that could entail.

The Great One had *political hay* riding on this particular patient, and he could also visualize one big medical malpractice suit staring him in the face. So he kept the patient under anesthesia and replaced the diseased mitral valve with a Starr-Edwards valve, which looks like a miniature Ping-Pong ball in a metal cage. It was *state-of-the-art* for 1972.

Stanton chose the mechanical valve rather than the more common tissue valve from a pig because of the patient's history of scleroderma morphia, which could conceivably attack the tissue valve replacement.

Stanton put his personal reputation over the welfare of the patient, an outrageous violation of his Hippocratic Oath and the tenets of the medical profession. He was chagrined that his arch-rival, Dr. Joseph Cleary, was the one to rescue him from losing the patient, which probably would have been a blessing for the female patient. As it turned out, she did suffer brain damage. Wally Deer had killed her on the table that day, but it took two more, hard, slow, terrible years for her to die.

As the Teller of Tales, I feel compelled to inject the truth in an otherwise, occasionally deceitful world.

If the operation itself was not bad enough, The Great One felt compelled to lie about it to the patient's family, telling them after surgery that everything went fine and the patient was doing well.

Stanton was saying the same thing three days later when the patient was still comatose. Stanton ordered the staff not to talk about the operation when the family started asking some pointed questions. Stanton was running scared, and Wally Deer was taken off the surgery schedule.

Despite Stanton's stonewalling attempts, the word got around the medical community about what happened. Stanton was furious. Then, for reasons perhaps only Dr. Rosie Willett could explain, Stanton seemed to blame Joe for his troubles, and that was the beginning of the major rift between them. Stanton released an official response to an enquiry from the University's Board of Trustees about Deer's resignation, an unusual event. In his resignation letter, Wally Deer had mentioned fatigue from long hours required by the residency program.

Dear Board of Trustees:

    Due to unfounded rumors surrounding the recent resignation of Dr. Walter Deer from the Cardiovascular Residency program, I feel compelled to clarify the situation. Dr. Deer's resignation was caused by the recent infraction of medical protocols during surgery on my patient. If those had been followed, the accident would not have happened.
    As for my decision to replace the mitral valve, that was a professional judgement based upon my many years of experience in cardio-vascular surgery. There are only two surgeons in the world who have performed more cardiac operations.
    The accusation that I tried to cover up the problem is not well-founded. It is a doctor's duty to relieve anxiety of the family of critical ill patients. It I had told the patient's family that a mistake had been made, it would not have helped the patient and would have greatly, and unnecessarily, upset the family.

Sincerely,

Theodore Stanton, M.D.
Dean, School of Medicine

Following the Deer incident, the relations between Ted Stanton and Joe Cleary went rapidly down hill. As Joe's fame and patient list increased, so did Stanton's blood pressure. Fortunately, their disagreements did not escape the walls of the medical school as happened with the 40-year feud between the great heart surgeons, Michael DeBakey and Denton Cooley, widely reported in the news media.

Even in his exalted position, Stanton had to be careful. Along with Joe's skill in surgery was his skill in raising money for medical research. He was the one man on the medical school faculty that could pick up a telephone and within minutes get pledges for a million dollars. Given a little time, he could increase that to ten million. In a research university, money talks, loudly, and money is power. I guess that isn't so different from anywhere else.

* * * * * *

It was just a few days after Frank had read Joe's proposed protocol for his project that I overheard a conversation between them.

Frank was saying, "Look, Joe, I believe in this research. You have convinced me that we can make a significant contribution to medicine, but let's be real, Ted Stanton is going to fight us on this one. He may also get support. This *is* probably the most radical research request in the history of the University, maybe any university. Don't you think for one moment that Stanton won't jump to cut you down to size whenever he sees an opportunity, and this project will give him that chance. He'll be after the jugular."

"I understand the problem, Frank. Ted's a fine surgeon, but if he starts trying to cut throats, just remember, he is only one member of a nine member committee, and remember that some scalpels have a double edge."

Chapter 4

The *Human Subjects Committee* is just the renamed *Research Committee* that was formed at the same time the Medical School was established twenty-five years earlier. Along came the bureaucrats from the Federal Department of Health and Human Services, *HUD*, in all of their Washington wisdom, and imposed severe restrictions on medical schools use of humans in experiments with the threat of cutting off Federal funding for violators of their onerous regulations. In defense of the bureaucrats, their collective memories were still conscious of the horrors of Nazi and Japanese medical experiments when the Department was formed in 1953.

The intent was good, the practice burdensome. If you wanted to do any research that even remotely involved a human in the process, Federal approval was required. The exception was made in certain cases, but to qualify for an exception, the universities, as well as drug companies, research hospitals and companies engaged in human research, were required to establish a *Human Subjects Committee* whose sole purpose was to evaluate the efficacy, safety, scientific purpose of the project, and whether it met Federal guidelines.

Dr. Ted Stanton had appointed himself as Chair of the Committee when he was selected as Dean of the Medical School, thus gaining even further power over the professional faculty and non-faculty professionals associated with the University. I repeat myself, *Money is power*.

Frank Picariello was pessimistic as usual about their chances before the Committee. Joe Cleary was enthusiastic and optimistic as usual. The Committee normally deliberated without the research team present, but in this case, most of the Committee members indicated they had questions to ask the team.

Besides Doctors Cleary and Picariello, the other team members that Joe had recruited were Dr. Rosamond Willett, Psychiatrist, introduced earlier; Dr. Albert Settleman, a Professor of Psychology, who would design part of the team's verification experiments; and Dr. William *Bill* Ryder, the team's general surgeon. They intended to add some other specialist later, such as a Perfusionist.

"Good morning," Dr. Stanton greeted the assemblage after they had filed into the conference room at the hospital and were settled at the table. The room was not as sparse as the offices, but it certainly did not exude extravagance. A long, boat shaped wooden table was occupied by the nine members of the Committee, who sat on wooden chairs with maroon cushions embroidered with the University's crest, the only concession to opulence. In the center of the table was a silver colored thermos of water on a tray with ten glasses.

A life-size oil portrait of the late Anthony Gilmore occupied a side wall. His widow donated the funds to build the hospital portion of the medical school which was named for him. On the opposite wall were numerous plaques indicating awards given to the Medical School.

The team took the empty chairs along the walls of the room. There was only one empty chair at the table reserved for the guest presenter. It was known among the staff as *The Hot Seat*.

"Dr. Cleary, please take the chair at the table," Stanton invited as Joe started to sit along the wall. It sounded more like a command than an invitation. The Great One was always formal in public, and I suspect he was not inclined towards too much civility towards Joe. The atmosphere was charged as Stanton had been working on the Committee before the team arrived.

"You know how we work," Stanton said as Joe sat down at the table, "and we have all read your protocol, so I'll dispense with the usual preliminaries and get right to the questions. I know the Committee has a few."

Stanton had a sonorous voice that matched his girth, and this always helped him dominate meetings. His voice could cancel the chatter of almost anyone who challenged him for attention. He was using it now.

"Dr. Cleary, it is only fair to warn you that the Committee has serious reservations about your proposed project. First, and not withstanding what you said in your protocol, it is not clear to us how your research into the death state has any direct bearing on the practice of medicine.

"Second, even if there was an application to medical practice, the Committee does not see a connection to the Division of Thoracic Surgery. Science cannot be expected to answer every conceivable question, and the question of such a transcendent subject as death is certainly one of those. Would you care to comment?"

Joe did not need to refer to notes to respond, but he opened his folder and picked up papers as if referring to notes. Over the years, Joe had learned to carefully weigh every question before replying to this Committee's questions. Stanton often loaded his questions with a trap. After a full minute of silence, during which The Great One began to fidget, Joe responded in his quiet, nonemotional and professional tone that he used with patients.

"Dr. Stanton, Committee members, the human body is but the shell of our true existence. What makes us unique as human beings is our spirit, our mind if you will, our personality, the psyche, call it what you will. No two humans are identical in that regard. Yet the medical profession knows little about, spends less time studying, and shows a certain disdain for research into the nonmaterial world of the mind. Our team Psychiatrist, Dr. Rosamond Willett can attest to that.

"If our team can demonstrate scientifically and conclusively that the human being is more than a physical body, but also contains a second, unseen body we call the psyche, then we will revolutionize psychological and physiological science. I am sure that Dr. Bernstein would agree."

Isaac Bernstein was the Chairman of the Department of Psychiatry and a member of the Committee. He nodded affirmatively as Joe spoke. Isaac was not a handsome man, short, squat, with angular face features, large nose, a thin salt and pepper beard, thin hair and a brilliant mind. He was a gentle person, well thought of by the staff and students, and a highly recognized leader in his field. He was also Rosie's boss. Joe knew how to play to the different members of the Committee. He could count on Isaac's vote.

"Considering the research that has been done at several U. S. and foreign universities," Joe continued, "we are convinced that the psyche in man is independent of the body for its existence. Even our own limited exposure to so-called *near-death experiences* has convinced us that the psyche does not cease to exist with the death of the body. As I once read, *Death is the ultimate fact of life, not merely the end of it.*

Stanton interrupted. "But Doctor, we know all this. No one will argue with you, although there may be a few agnostics around who would challenge the *life after death* hypothesis.

The question is, what has all of this got to do with medicine? Our job is to sustain life, not explain death."

"I was about to get to that point, Dr. Stanton, and you are right. In simple terms our job as physicians is to sustain life, but the question I ask all of you is, what is life?

"The medical profession, religious leaders and even the citizenry cannot even agree on when life begins, and we know that our profession has changed dramatically over the years in defining when life ends. Despite all of our amazing advances in the medical field, we still cannot answer those questions with absolute certainty.

"There are educated people who still say that life begins with the delivery of a child into the waiting arms of its mother, notwithstanding the detection of a heart beat as early as twenty-one days after conception.

"We have brought forth human life in test tubes. We regularly perform surgery on fetuses only months old. Our medical scientists are changing the genes of unborn children, even before life as we know it. We are very much involved with life before life.

"Death? The body dies, but when? We are all old enough to remember when we believed life ended when the heart and lungs stopped functioning, at least for legal and medical purposes. Now, we can detect signs of electrical activity in the heart as long as forty minutes after it has stopped beating.

"Today we can keep the body alive when the brain is dead, or at least when we think it is dead. The concept of *brain death* is of recent construct, a product of the mid-1960s. If the body is alive, what is it that makes the brain dead? How does a body function without a live brain? Solely by our modern machinery? As a scientist, I wonder.

"You, colleagues and Committee members, are well aware of the debate that rages among the bioethicists and the medical profession. Some say that death should include those who have no brain functions, the so-called *brain dead*. That became the definition of death in 1968. The unsettled nature of when a person is dead was carried to an extreme in Sweden as late as 1985, last year, when the question arose whether the recipient of an artificial heart might be termed legally dead under Swedish law.

"Others say that death should also include those who have lost complete consciousness, the *cognitive dead*, those in a persistent vegetative state.

"As an interesting aside, and as you may have read, there are Yogis that can temporarily stop their hearts and breathing, and then assume a trancelike state that resembles physical death, at least that which we are calling *cognitive death*. There are recorded cases where this death like state has been maintained for days. The Yogis explain they withdraw *life energy* from the body and concentrate it into the brain. Only enough *life energy* remains in the body to keep it from decaying. We have much to learn from Eastern philosophy and practice.

"My colleagues and I are suggesting as a premise in our Protocol that death of the physical human being occurs when the nonphysical psyche permanently leaves its physical body host.

"It is our belief that the time has come, facing the reality of what is happening to our patients, when we must consider the possibility and potentialities *that death is no longer a final barrier to life*. The question that is really being debated, colleagues and friends, is not when does life begin, nor when it ends, but what is it?

"In his *Discoveries on Method,* Descartes said, *Doubt everything. Take as false what was probable, to take as probable what was called certain, and to reject all else.* If my team's hypothesis is true, that the psyche is an essential, functional part of human existence, independent of brain activity, the implications to medical science are profound. Life and death will have to be redefined. Death has a meaning of *finality*, but if the spirit, the mind, the psyche, *or the soul* as some call it, is immutable, then we must reexamine the entire spectrum of medical care and ethics.

"Medical practitioners are aware of mankind's fear of death, the emotional problems of the patient and family alike, and the dire need for us to cope with these problems in our practice.

"Everything associated with death has negative connotations, something frightening and evil, a very lonely process at best. Yet, every living being will face this hooded adversary. Modern science cannot provide an escape from death's inevitability, but can provide knowledge to erase the fear. Fear of the unknown has always limited discovery, and death is the last great medical frontier.

"In the medical profession, death is often considered a defeat, a kind of insult to professional competence. There is still something of a shock to hospital staffs when a patient dies, like the death is a personal affront, a personal failure.

"Although compassion and conscientiousness to duty are admirable traits, we must not assume attitudes of guilt that cause us to shun terminal patients or to cease our care. Our profession must be trained to deal with death just as we are trained to work with the natural functions of life. We must be ready to aid our patients in the transition from this world to the next, not in a philosophical or religious sense, but in a scientific sense."

Joe paused from his long speech as he took a paper from the stack in front of him. Despite his long exposition, he had the full attention of the Committee. Even Stanton showed interest. Joe took a sip of water, then continued as he read from the paper.

"In his posthumously published autobiography, Carl Jung said, *Death is psychologically just as important as birth, an integral part of life. It is not the psychologist who must question as to what happens finally to the detached consciousness. Whatever theoretical position he assumes, he would hopelessly overstep the boundaries of his scientific competence. . . As physician, then, I make the greatest effort to fortify, so far as I have the power, a belief in immortality, especially in my older patients whom such questions come menacingly near.*

"My colleagues, have we so quickly forgotten the admonition of Maimonides?" and Joe picked up another paper from the table and read from the 12th Century Jewish philosopher, Maimonides, whose prayer has been read at one time or another by every physician. Joe read the prayer.

Enlighten my mind that it may recognize what presents itself, and that it may comprehend what is absent or hidden. Let it not fail to see what is visible, but do not permit it to arrogate to itself the power to see what cannot be seen for delicate and indefinite are the bounds of the great art of caring for the lives and health of Your creatures . . . Almighty God, You have chose me in Your mercy to watch over the life and death of Your creatures.

"Members of the Committee, we do well in watching over the lives of those entrusted to our care. We are merely suggesting, supported by Carl Jung and Maimonides, that we have more work to do to watch over their deaths.

Chapter 5

Doctors Cleary and Picariello had their hands full with the Human Subjects Committee. As the Teller of Tales, I am but a humble observer of events, and better qualified to make impersonal observations of the behavior of humans than either of them. What is that expression that humans often use, *I've got no dog in the fight*? I digress.

Dr. Joseph Cleary's presentation had a definite effect on the Committee judging from the expressions on their faces. Mostly good, except for Theodore Stanton, who was showing agitation because he wasn't hearing the words he wanted to hear. He was also aware of the other Committee members' looks of approval. His feelings came through in his response.

"Dr. Cleary, I am certain that all of your colleagues here remember Maimonides prayer, but I fail to see what significance that has upon my previous questions. The philosophy of death is hardly a subject for the medical school, and particularly for the Thoracic Surgery Division. It would be better addressed by the social scientists of the School of Arts and Sciences, or the Department of Philosophy, or even the Department of Theology.

"Answers you seek cannot be validated out of empirical experience. You seek answers to questions that belong in the province of religion, myth, metaphysics or imaginative literature, wouldn't you agree?"

A question like that I feared would cause Joe's Irish blood to boil over into verbal confrontation. If so, that would hurt his team's chances with the Committee.

As for Stanton, how could one person be so positive in his belief while so ignorant of the facts? But that is Stanton. The expression on Dr. Frank Picariello's face looked as if he were trying to tell Joe by telepathy to count to ten before replying, hoping that Joe would remember Frank's earlier warning.

Maybe Joe got the message because his face retained the passive, unemotional look for several seconds. Then his lower lip pursed the way that a child sometimes does in a stubborn mood. Joe's look was really one of contemplation, not stubbornness. Over the centuries, it has been my observation that *the intensity of one's determination can often move mountains of resistance, or create grand illusions of success.* Which was it to be? Joe provided the answer.

"You may be right, Dr. Stanton. Perhaps the social scientists, the philosophers, the theologians, are the appropriate ones to consider death. They do, in fact, extensively. *However*," and Joe placed emphasis on the word and a slight pause, "social scientists, philosophers and theologians do not deal with death on a daily basis. We do. This week alone, eighteen people have died in this hospital for various reasons. How many died in Benedict Hall?" and Joe was referring to the Social Sciences building on campus.

"Only Oncology sees more deaths than Thoracic Surgery. Death is not a parochial issue. We have no medical department with a monopoly on death. As for the psyche, Dr. Bernstein could rightfully claim that subject for his Department of Psychiatry, but the death rate of his patients caused by their illnesses is not statistically significant. We have Dr. Willett from his staff on our team as you know.

"A final point, if I may. Some of the finest research in this country on the subject of near-death experiences has been done by M. B. Salome, an M.D. at the Veterans Hospital in Atlanta, and by a fellow Georgian, Dr. Raymond Moody. Both have written scholarly papers and books on the subject. Dr. Salome is a cardiologist. Dr. Moody is both a PhD in Psychology and an M.D. He devotes his entire practice to near-death cases. We would be willing to expand our team to include other medical departments should this be considered prudent by the Committee."

Joe looked around the table, but no Committee member volunteered, so he continued his presentation of the Protocol.

"We are very much aware that our proposed project entails basic research, and its contribution to any particular aspect of medicine is unknown. That is the nature of basic research, as you are all well aware, the pursuit of knowledge without the restraints of prescribed end objectives."

Richard Ingersoll, a non medic, Comptroller of the Medical School, leaned forward, looking at Joe and asked, "Dr. Cleary, you are considered in the profession, and certainly here on campus, as one of the leading thoracic and cardiovascular surgeons in the nation, if not the world. I am more concerned with you being the subject of the research than I am of the research itself. Can't you find someone else to be the subject? I do believe there is some prohibition against experiments where a high probability of death is present. Finally, how do you propose to pay for this project?"

Let me tell you, reader of this tale, Ted Stanton wasn't too happy to hear those words from Dick Ingersoll, one of the senior citizens on the staff who technically worked for Stanton, but in reality had a direct pipeline to the University Comptroller and the Chancellor, a situation well-understood by Stanton. Ingersoll's statement about Joe being *one of the outstanding thoracic and cardiovascular surgeons in the world* was placing Joe and Stanton on the same level. Stanton was grinding his teeth to control his feelings.

Ingersoll did have a debt to Stanton. He was a fixture around the campus, predating the establishment of the Medical School. Stanton used his influence to keep Ingersoll on the job after Ingersoll had reached the mandatory retirement age. It was some kind of contract situation after *official* retirement. Stanton's motive was not benevolent, but more self-serving in that Dick Ingersoll had strong ties to the University's Comptroller, and hence, money. Stanton considered Ingersoll's words as a betrayal.

It was Stanton that had earlier planted the seed in the Committee members' minds that perhaps Joe's intrigue with death might have something to do with the loss of his wife and daughter, implying that Joe may be trying to commit legal suicide. It wasn't stated, but the idea was out there. That may have prompted Ingersoll's question. Of course, Frank Picariello had the same thought when Joe had broached the research to him, but Frank had dismissed it quickly. Joe answered Ingersoll's question.

"You can understand, Mr. Ingersoll, that I have given *that* subject a great deal of attention. I may be a curious scientist - is there any other kind - but I hope that I am also a prudent one. I understand the risks as well as anyone, and contrary to any other opinion, I have no desire to prove the cliché that *curiosity killed the cat!*"

Joe's comment suggested that he knew there was speculation that he was morbid about the deaths of Linda and Becky. Joe continued.

"I'll address the second part of your question first, Mr. Ingersoll, about experiments that may lead to death. What you are probably referring to is the *Nuremberg Code*. The Code was the first formal treatment of the subject of getting permission from the subjects of experiments. I knew this might come up, and I have a copy of the pertinent section with me." With that, Joe began looking through his briefcase, and finally found what he was looking for.

"Here, in Article 5, it states, *No experiment should be conducted where there is an 'a-priori' reason to believe that death or disabling injury will occur; except, perhaps,* and I wish to emphasize the next statement, *in those experiments where the experimental physicians also serve as the subjects.* Since I am the *experimental physician*, I am well within the intent of the code, and in my opinion, within the ethics of a research scientist.

"As for the first part of your question, *Why me?* I can only refer you to the fact that self-experimentation in the medical field has a long and noble history. I know that medical members of the Committee are aware of this, but for the benefit of the lay members, let me elucidate.

"In preparation for this meeting, I reviewed the research on using yourself as a subject of research. I learned something for my effort. I was surprised to find that an Italian, a Sixteenth-Seventeenth Centuries medical doctor named Santorio Santorio is credited with the first recorded self-experiments. Some of his findings were published in the early Seventeenth Century book, *De Statica Medicina.* He was a pioneer in collecting medical statistics.

"So you see, self-experimentation is hardly a new idea. Who knows, the redundancy in his name may have started the whole idea of double-blind tests in research!"

Joe looked up from his notes, and the corners of his mouth wrinkled in a tight little grin. He was trying to inject humor into his somber subject. He got a few polite grins. Frank did not think it was that amusing, but then he had learned to smile at his friend's jokes. Besides, he never liked Italian jokes.

Frank thought to himself, *As a comedian, it is a good thing Joe became a surgeon.* Dr. Joe continued.

"I know you will be happy to hear, Mr. Ingersoll, that I will not be asking for University funds for the project. It will be self-financed by my task force. I am personally investing two million dollars, and Doctors Picariello and Willett one million each. Should we need more, I am confident we can find the money outside of University funding.

"Let me return to your more serious concern about my being the subject of our experiment. If it were not for self-experimentation, the world might not have morphine, or Jenner's smallpox vaccine, or rabies vaccine, or even cyclosporine that Doctor Stanton and other transplant surgeons rely upon to fight tissue rejection. These are all products of self-experimentation, as is one the cardiologist's and thoracic surgeon's most valuable tool, cardiac catheterization.

"Perhaps our biggest problem for selecting a subject for our experiment, Mr. Ingersoll, was to find someone who was not only willing, but is scientifically trained. I suppose, given time, we could find other subjects. I have enough confidence in our team that planned trips to the beyond will be less risky than your morning commute on the freeway." Joe's lips registered his second thin smile.

Dick Ingersoll sounded satisfied with Joe's answer. "I believe that what I am hearing you say, Dr. Cleary, is that curiosity may have killed the cat, but *satisfaction brought it back.* Let us hope that we can bring you back."

"I have a question for you, Dr. Cleary, if I may," Dr. James Klinger interposed.

As the Teller of Tales, I need to again digress from my story a moment to explain that the *Human Subjects Committee* has five M.D.s, including Stanton the Chair. Along with the medical doctors, there were the Director of the Pharmacology Department; Director of the Nursing School; a nonvoting student member, and in this case a second-year medical student; the Medical School's Comptroller; and one public member. The present public member was a woman in her mid-forties, prominent in the community and an alumnus of the University.

The four other M.D.s change according to the subject of the protocol being offered, or, as in the case of Dr. Jim Klinger, a Pediatrician, whoever on the panel was available. For this meeting, the other physicians were Psychiatrist Isaac Bernstein, previously introduced; Doctor Carl Rogers, Director of Internal Medicine; and Dr. Vladimir Panofsky, Director of the Orthopedic Department.

Dr. Jim Klinger's voice was as soft as his manner. He was a gentle man and had chosen a specialty that matched his demeanor - Pediatrics. Jim was fifty-five, a grandfather, originally from South Carolina, and the resident *Southern Gentleman,* although a disheveled one. His wrinkled suits were an ill-fit for his skinny frame. His long, white ruffled hair was a favorite target for kid's hands. The loose tie and scuffed shoes all contributed to the name give to him by his children patients, *Scarecrow*. Klinger's smile was as contagious as measles, his wit as sharp as a scalpel, and his love of children as great as his considerable skill.

The love was returned by patient and parents alike. Dr. Klinger was one of those in the Medical School responsible for getting the Ronald McDonald House built at the hospital for parents of terminally ill children in order for them to stay with their child during treatment. It was modeled after the first one built at Stanford University.

Dr. Klinger's research into the effects of malnutrition on the growth of children had placed him in demand around the world. His favorite saying, hanging on his office wall, was, *There is more cure in an ounce of love than a ton of pills.*

"Dr. Cleary, *suh*," Klinger said with his slow, soft, Southern drawl, "with all due respect to the competency of your team, and apologies for my seeming ignorance, it is not clear to me from your proposal exactly how you as the subject will be put into the brain-dead condition without some permanent damage to yourself. Of course, that assumes it is possible to resuscitate you from that condition. Would you care to elaborate?"

"If you don't mind, Dr. Klinger, I am going to let Dr. Frank Picariello, my co-director, explain that to you. Dr. Picariello has developed that part of the research. Frank?"

Chapter 6

Dr. Frank Picariello chose to remain seated in his chair against the wall as he arranged the pages in his notebook. He was prepared for the question, assuming someone would ask.

"Putting a person to death is not a technical problem as you know, Dr. Klinger," Frank began. "Putting a person to death with the intention of resuscitating without injury to the brain or causing a dysfunction of some kind *is* a technical challenge.

"Our first thought was that we could induce brain death by drugs. As most of you are aware, there are numerous drugs that will paralyze the respiratory system, *Curare, Pancuronium, Metocurine, Vecuronium* are a few that come to mind. For the most part, these drugs do not cause brain dysfunction unless the patient is not adequately ventilated, or the drugs are given in an overdose. That could cause irreversible damage.

"There are also the better-known hallucinogenic drugs such as *lysergic acid diethyl-amide*, the infamous LSD, or *mescaline* and *ketamine*. These could induce death.

"There are negatives in the use of these drugs for our research. They may have an adverse affect upon the experiments, leaving open that any findings reported by the subject could be rightfully questioned whether he was suffering from a hallucination or reporting a true experience.

Barbiturates would probably do the job, but they would also imperil the credibility of the experiments.

"The team decided to rule out any drugs that might introduce anomalies into the experiments. We prefer to induce brain death and cardiac arrest with the least amount of trauma.

"Having ruled out drugs, we had few options open. Then one day, Bill Ryder," and Frank quickly added, "Dr. Ryder, who we introduced earlier and is with us today, suggested that we should cool the subject to slow the metabolism until the subject was on a flat." Frank was again referring to the Electroencephalogram trace. He continued.

"Reducing the metabolism as most of you know, reduces the brain's and other cell's need for oxygen. That gave me an idea. I had just recently read in one of the journals about the work a small group of scientists were doing at the University of California in reducing the temperature of primates, in this case a Chimpanzee, to 3° Celsius, which, of course, caused a flat and a cardiac arrest. After an hour in that state, these researchers were able to bring the Chimp back to normal without any apparent physiological problems. They had been doing the same thing for several years with dogs and hamsters.

"I thought, why couldn't we do the same with a human subject? Chimpanzees are a close physiological relative to man. The UC scientists had developed techniques for preventing ice crystals from forming in the blood at such low temperatures. Of course, we would not need such low temperature to obtain cardiac arrest in a human subject. It looked promising.

"The lower temperatures would significantly reduce the oxygen requirements for the brain, and we would not have to introduce drugs into the subject's system of the type that could cloud the outcome of the experiment. A final benefit, there would be no new technology involved."

Dr. Klinger interjected another question. "Excuse me, Dr. Picariello, but has this procedure ever been attempted on a human subject by the UC researchers or anyone else? I rather suspect not from what you said. Only primates, is that right?"

"That is correct, Dr. Klinger. We do not know of any low temperature experiments on humans. However, there are many cases where there have been hypothermia-induced deaths and the victims were resuscitated without any apparent damage. One such case involved a deliberate attempt by physicians to separate Siamese twins by reducing their temperature. I'll speak to that in a moment.

"I researched the subject and found that the longest recorded time a human was clinically dead as a result of hypothermia, and later revived, happened to a seven-year old Swedish girl. She drowned in the freezing waters of a lake, and was in the death state in the water for an hour before she was rescued and resuscitated, apparently without damage. It is obvious the lowered temperatures, in this case 13° Celsius, or 55.4° Fahrenheit, a record, helped slow down the girl's metabolism so that the brain did not demand the normal amount of oxygen.

"There is also the case last year of then two-and a half year old Michael Troche of Milwaukee. He wandered outside wearing nothing but his pajamas and diaper into below 20° Fahrenheit weather. They were not certain whether he had been outside for thirty minutes or three hours because of the circumstances, but when he was found his body temperature was 60° Fahrenheit, 15.55° Celsius, and he was clinically dead. Dr. Kevin Kelly, the attending physician said, *When he came into the hospital, the legs and arms felt like blocks of ice, and as you squeezed the tissue, you could feel ice in the blood, as you would crush ice under the skin.* After heroic efforts at the hospital, little Michael's heart began to beat. After a long recuperation, he returned to normal.

"There was another, similar case that happened in Chicago some years ago when a nine-year old boy fell into Lake Michigan. He was in the water for at least ten to fifteen minutes, and when they got him out he had no pulse and his body temperature was 13.5° Celsius, close to the Swedish girl's temperature. He was resuscitated and did not suffer any long term effects.

"The technique of using hypothermia as an adjunct in surgery goes back centuries, but has never been in general use. I mentioned Siamese twins earlier. Here are the details. Recently at John Hopkins, seven-month old Siamese twins, joined at the head, had their temperature reduced to 21.5° Celsius, 70.7°Fahrenheit, and then their blood was removed and surgery successfully performed to separate them. Hypothermia was the crucial element. We are comfortable with our decision."

Jim Klinger was satisfied with Dr. Picariello's response, so Frank continued explaining how the research team planned to place Joe Cleary into a death state.

"There are a number of techniques for lowering the body temperature that have been used in the operating room, including ice packs. After reviewing the methods and equipment available, we decided to prevail upon friends in the School of Engineering to design a new piece of equipment for the purpose. They have obliged, and we plan to use it. They call their device a *Refrigerated and Warming Dewar*, RWD for short. For those not familiar with the term *Dewar*, it is the name of the Scottish chemist and physicist that invented the vacuum bottle. His name is now applied to any double clad containers with a vacuum between the layers to keep liquids inside at set ambient temperatures, low or high.

"Our Dewar will be in the shape of a coffin, and I know that is a terrible term for this effort, but the shape is appropriate. It will have the necessary electronics, refrigeration and heating elements, all fully controllable. This will give us absolute control over the subjects environment, a critical component when involving human subjects. The RWD also serves as an operating table, and when its transparent hood is raised, it has all the necessary features of a fully functional operating table.

"We originally believed we would introduce a *perfluorocarbon*, such as *perfluorodeclin*, to insure an adequate supply of oxygen to the blood. After discussing this with cryogenic scientists at UC Berkeley, it was decided that at the low temperatures we anticipate, and the short duration in the Omega state, oxygen levels would not be a major problem.

"While I'm on the subject, I'll explain the resuscitation plans. It will be essentially the reverse process. We will warm Dr. Cleary's blood through the heart-lung machine. The refrigeration component of the RWD will be reversed to the heating elements so that instead of cryogenic cooling liquids running through the tubing, hot water will be used. When the body temperature has risen to about 30° to 32° Celsius, 82° to 89° Fahrenheit, or somewhere in that range, almost impossible to predict, we expect that the subject's heart will start beating by itself. If not, we will be prepared to restart the heart using cardioversion by either the direct injection of *Epinephrine*, or electric shock. The team also expects brain waves to begin registering as the temperature rises.

"After a set period, if there is still no brain activity, we will then resort to stimulants, although we consider this a remote possibility."

Dr. Klinger had a final follow-up question. "Dr. Picariello, the process of lowering the body temperature to such extreme lows will cause significant discomfort to the subject. If you are not going to use drugs, how will you lessen the pain and problems associated with Dr. Cleary descending into hypothermia?"

"Good point, Dr. Klinger, and thank you for reminding me. As we said, Dr. Rosamond Willett is on our team. She is a qualified hypnotist, and she plans to hypnotize Dr. Cleary before lowering his body temperature. She is confident this will eliminate all feeling by hypnotic suggestion. She also hopes that Dr. Cleary will respond to her commands to reenter his body after a set time." That answer seemed to satisfy Dr. Klinger.

Frank Picareillo had a brief thought about his and Joe's recent conversation in Frank's kitchen about Rosie Willett's hypnosis versus Frank's *gasses*.

Dr. Maynard Kyle, PhD, Director of the Pharmacology Department, a reticent sort of fellow, raised his hand slightly, no higher than his chest, enough to get Frank's attention. Frank asked, "You have a question, Dr. Kyle?"

"Dr. Picariello, how long will the subject be kept in the Omega or flatline state once it is attained?"

Frank deferred to Joe to answer.

Joe responded, "On the first attempt, Maynard, we will start resuscitation within five minutes after achieving a flat. The time for subsequent experiments will be determined by the results of the previous test, but we have in mind short durations of several minutes during the first part of our research. We want to get the techniques of obtaining a flat and resuscitation mastered before we venture into deeper waters so to speak. I can assure you that we will proceed with great caution. There is much at stake, including my life!"

Chapter 7

Chairman Stanton called a ten-minute break. Coffee was brought into the room along with an assortment of cookies. The Committee was an hour into the meeting. It was a few minutes past 10:00 AM and Stanton wanted to complete the meeting before a noon lunch. He called the meeting back to order quickly, and suggested the attendees continue to drink their coffee.

Dr. Carl Rogers, Director of the Internal Medicine Department held his hand up and was recognized by the Chairman. Rogers was a scholar and fine diagnostician. Along with Dr. Joe Cleary, Rogers was one of the youngest to head a major department, in his early forties, but he had established his intellectual prowess at an early age. He finished medical school when he was twenty-one years old.

A bachelor, Carl Rogers was too busy for a personal life, much to the dismay of many young women at the University. He was known for his perceptive approach to every problem, whether medical, teaching, or personal. There was a certain amount of haughtiness about him, and a tendency to be impatient with those who did not follow his rationale quickly enough. He was a little like Joe Cleary in that regard.

Rogers said, "That was a very interesting discourse, Dr. Picariello, but my question is for Dr. Cleary." He turned to Joe and dropped the formal titles. "You raised an interesting point in your Protocol, Joe, about near-death experiences. As I see it, one of the research problems will be to establish some form of a double-blind test that will give credibility to any of your findings, and it may require more than a double name like Santorio Santorio as Frank mentioned."

There were a few smiles. Rogers continued.

"For example, if you are successful in duplicating the experiences of near-death, similar to those reported in the literature, how will you be able to have independent verification? I am not suggesting any *skullduggery* mind you, and I know you have considered this in your Protocol, but you did not elaborate and it is not clear. Could you comment a little further?"

"Of course, Carl, I would be happy to. You are correct. It was an oversight on our part not to elaborate. We were a little rushed to get the Protocol ready for this meeting and did not give Dr. Willett, who is handling this for us, adequate time to do a thorough job. Verification of the experiment is part of her assignment on the team. If you don't mind, I will ask Dr. Willett to fill-in the details as to where we are today."

Dr. Rosamond Willett reached into her briefcase and removed several sheets of paper. Joe got up from his chair at the table and motioned for Rosie to take it.

"Dr. Rogers and Committee Members," Rosie began,"the team had decided to solicit the aid of Professor Albert Settleman of the Department of Psychology as a member of our team. Many of you know him and he is with us today. You may also recall that Dr. Settleman is the University's leading educator and authority in the field of parapsychology. He is a distinguished graduate of Duke University's School of Parapsychology where he studied under Dr. J. B. Rhine.

"Dr. Settleman and I, after much research and discussion, decided that the best method to test the validity of the subject reaching an out-of-body state would be to devise a double-blind test, double-blind in the sense that no member of the team, including myself, would know what test had been devised with one exception. Only Dr. Settleman and his assistant, Adrienne Henry, will develop, administer and know the details of the test. Ms. Henry is not a member of the team, but has been Dr. Settleman's assistant for over ten years. She has an MS in statistics."

"What I understand you to say, Dr. Willett, is that the tests are confidential to two people, and that we will not know the validity of the verification tests themselves until the experiment is complete. Is that correct?" Dr. Roger's asked.

"Yes, except that Professor Settleman intends to leave sealed packages with the test plans inside with the Chancellor of the University, Dean of the Medical School and with the President of the Faculty Senate. After each experiment, the results of the verification tests will be given to the Human Subjects Committee, together with the sealed test plan envelope. The Committee can then open the envelope and compare the plan with the results.

"I see," a still somewhat skeptical Dr. Rogers responded, "although I think this a rather unusual method of blind testing."

"We aren't testing drugs as you do in your Department, Dr. Rogers," Dr. Willett explained. "There is no placebo in death. No one plays dead in this scenario. Professor Settleman would only tell us that he will devise tests that challenge the subject to identify certain things that occur *after* the subject is placed in the zero brain wave state. It is the Professor who suggested we stop using the term *death* in our project, since it connotes finality. He suggested we develop a more scientific term such as *Omega Syndrome*. Since Omega is the twenty-fourth and last letter of the Greek alphabet, and has frequently represented death, the team elected to take Professor Settleman's advice."

Rosie handled herself very well and the Committee seemed pleased. However, as I looked around the room, there was one Committee member who had been sitting at the table, silent, intent, but constantly twiddling his pencil as if it were a bone he was going to break and reset just for the practice.

Dr. Vladimir Panofsky was an Orthopedic Surgeon and Director of the Orthopedic Division. A bear of a man, he looked as if he could break bones as well as fix them. It was difficult to comprehend that his large, beefy hands could handle the delicate surgical instruments of his specialty, but they did. He was a skillful surgeon.

His heavily bearded face always looked disturbed when he was listening intently, as he was now, adding substance to the name given to him by his students, *The Mad Russian*. He owed his Director's position to Stanton, and usually followed The Great One's lead.

Panofsky started tapping the eraser end of the pencil on the table as he directed a question to Joe. "Dr. Cleary, without debating the medical merits of your proposal, permit me to ask that with our present state of medical knowledge, aren't we best advised to leave spiritual matters to the clergy? Father McGuire does a fine job of consoling the patients who are terminal. Why can't we confine our skills to, if you'll excuse the commercial, mending bones?" Panofsky's deadpan attempt at humor gained him just a few smiles.

Joe smiled too. "Dr. Panofsky, you have really answered your own question. You are absolutely correct when you say we stick to practicing what we know because we don't know to do any better. We are proposing to *advance* the state of the medical arts, not be satisfied with the status quo. That's the whole purpose of basic research as this panel well knows."

I could see that Panofsky, who Joe had not met before, was about to raise an objection about the way Joe characterized his question, but Joe didn't give him a chance to break-in.

"My colleague, Dr. Picariello, raised a similar point when I first broached the project to him, the point about leaving death to the theologians. My reply then and my reply now is that is exactly what we have been doing since man started worshipping things he could not understand. He created gods and myths to explain the unexplainable. Our earliest healers were priests, although we called them witch doctors, sorcerers, magicians. If they couldn't heal with herbs or mud, they tried invoking their gods through incantations which became prayers. Even the ancients recognized there was some connection between healing and faith, mystery and power.

"As members of the Committee may recall from their own education, every culture has its own customs and beliefs. When unanswerable questions were raised in ancient cultures, those questions were often branded as subjects of shame or taboo and mystery, making the subjects unacceptable for discussion in the society. What the clergy itself could not explain, their followers were expected to *have faith*. This is the *ignorance is bliss* school of thought, and the population was conditioned to blindly follow the dictates of the leaders, who were either members of the clergy or who were strongly influenced by the clergy.

"When you think about it, we really haven't progressed very far in the philosophy of medicine. When we as the descendant practitioners of Hippocrates face death with our patients, we invoke the gods just like the witch doctors, and our incantation is, *Call Father McGuire*.

"I believe it is time to push our knowledge further. The only one who can lose on this project is me, but everyone in the whole world of today and tomorrow can gain. Those are rather good stakes, wouldn't you agree?

"I have no quarrel with the theologians, Dr. Panofsky, but I do not recognize their monopoly on death. If I can choose, I much prefer to meet the *God of Wisdom* than the *Devil of Ignorance.*"

The next question came from a surprising source, Henry Quincy, the second year Medical School student, the recently appointed student member of the Board. Student members were usually hesitant to speak, afraid they might demonstrate their ignorance to their detriment. Henry surprised himself.

"Dr. Cleary, if I may. If you have no inhibitions about treading upon the toes of our good Irish padre, have you considered the legal implications of having yourself killed, not only for yourself, but for those assisting you?"

I was a little surprised by Henry's question. He must have recently taken the course in Medical Ethics, judging from the nature of his question. Of course, as a Teller of Tales, I had thought about that issue myself, although I am reluctant to put my ideas into human brains, so I was interested to hear Joe's answer, which was quick in coming.

"That is a fair question," and I could see Joe look at the nameplate in front of the questioner. Ted Stanton had apparently assumed that everyone knew each other. "Mr. Quincy," Joe completed his sentence. "I have thought about it, yes, but dismissed it rather quickly. If no one is dead legally, there is no legal issue. I don't plan to be dead, or as the team prefers to say, in the Omega state for very long, certainly not long enough for someone to file charges." Joe smiled at what he meant to be a little humor.

"While I'm gone for a few minutes, who will make the determination that I am truly and legally dead? Remember my earlier comments about that.

"If by chance I cannot be recovered after being placed in the flatline status, it is an accident during a medical experiment. The worst that could happen would be a coroner's inquest, and we've been through that routine almost everyday. Accidents happen all the time in experiments, and people are killed. A new airplane, a new weapon, a new race car, a new drug. A little paperwork at worst."

"Could be, Joe," Richard Ingersoll, the Medical School Comptroller interjected, "but you are hardly a routine research subject. I don't want you asking for a higher salary, but after all, you *are* famous," he said with a try at humor, "and I really can't see that your death by *accident* would result in just 'a little more paperwork!'"

"I'll concede the point, Dick," and Joe dug the needle into The Great One by the continued informality, " and perhaps my permanent demise might result in a *lot* more paperwork, and maybe I should ask for a higher salary!"

That comment got the group to laugh, making Frank Picariello again wonder why people laugh at poor puns. Nevertheless, Joe was scoring points. Dick Ingersoll continued.

"Well, Joe, a higher salary isn't the problem. I note that you recently raised a half-million dollars from private sources for this project, so, no University funds are involved. Are you sure the money wouldn't be better spent on your Cardiovascular & Thoracic Research Center? They always seem to be underfunded." The Center was one of Joe's pet projects.

"Dick, you know that every department in the University always says it is underfunded. They are like giant vacuum machines, or Black Holes, sucking up every penny that comes their way. The CAT Center, as we call it, is endowed, and sure, they could always find uses for more funds, but the money I raised for this project is dedicated to the project and could not be used at the Center anyway. Funding is not the issue. Support by this Committee may be!"

Dr. Theodore Stanton had not been able to get a word in for fifteen minutes, and he was frustrated. Earlier he had appeared lost in thought. In my travels through time, I have often found that people get lost in thought because they are traveling in unfamiliar territory, and Stanton was no exception. He sensed a leaning of Committee members in favor of Joe's project. Now he saw a new lead, a new chance to block the proposal.

"Now, Dr. Cleary," he began as he injected formality back into the proceedings, with a tone of condescension, "Mr. Ingersoll's point is that we have so many demands for funds for worthwhile research programs that we must use great discretion and wisdom in placing priorities on these programs. We can't fund them all, and if money is not the issue, hospital facilities are likewise limited. Mr. Ingersoll is merely suggesting there may be other programs of higher medical interest that deserve the funding and facilities."

I knew how Joe would react. After all, I am the Teller of Tales. His face quickly lost his smile and turned sober and dispassionate. He paused again for a few seconds before responding.

"As I said, Dr. Stanton, the funds we have raised are earmarked for the project alone and cannot be diverted to other programs. That was the condition upon which they were donated. . . ."

Stanton interrupted Joe before he was finished with his thought. "I assume the donors' restrictions were at your urging, in which case, Doctor, I presume you could influence them to change their minds. I'm sure they would not mind transferring the funds to other of our worthwhile programs, or even to your Center, should the Committee elect not to approve this project."

My, my, even Stanton had overstepped. Some of his supporters on the Committee were taken back by Stanton's impugning of Joe's statement. The muscles tightened in Dr. Joe's throat and face as he fought back a rash response. His eyes, ah, his eyes, lost the moist glint of humor of seconds before, and had turned icy cold. Stanton had gone too far. Joe was mad. I could see that and so could Frank Picariello who was hoping Joe was counting to ten again before responding.

"I will repeat, Doctor Stanton, the funds are restricted to the program on the table before you. They will not be transferred to another. If the project cannot be pursued under the auspices of this University, then, members of the Committee, I am certain there are other universities that would jump at the chance."

Joe had laid down the gauntlet. I said earlier in the story that Joe was the biggest fund-raiser in the Medical School, outpacing Stanton by twenty-million dollars at Stanton's peak a few years before. During the past year alone, Joe had raised over fifty-million dollars for the hospital, research and resident scholarships. He did this by the strength of his reputation, and the confidence the donors had in him. The Departments of every member of the Committee had benefited financially from Joe's effort, and all of that suddenly came into focus by Joe's words. Stanton may have helped many of the Committee members to get to their present positions, but it was Joe's help in getting money that kept them in their jobs. So as far as Stanton's influence was concerned, it's the adage, *Don't tell me what you did for me yesterday, what have you done for me recently?* Gratitude is one favor long.

Dick Ingersoll, *Mr. Moneybags* himself, was the quickest to respond. "Hold on, Joe, I don't believe that Ted meant exactly what it sounded like. The Committee hasn't voted on the proposal yet. I'm sure that Ted was only reinforcing my point that we wanted to make sure that we are doing the job we are supposed to do, review these proposals as to their medical merit, protection of the human subject, and financial viability. Isn't that correct Ted?"

The manner in which Ingersoll said the last sentence clearly told The Great One to get in line because the University's Administration was going to back Joe. They could not literally afford to lose him. Even though Ted Stanton might be the Dean of the Medical School, the financial executive had unusual clout, usually on a par with any Dean and sometimes with the University President. Dr. Theodore Stanton was about to lose his first major bout with Joe, and he didn't like it one bit. He had to bite his lip as he responded.

"Of course, Dick, I only want us to do our job. I've always recognized the importance of breaking new ground, being on the leading edge of discovery, but within reasonable and practical limits."

Old Stanton was hedging, using tired clichés and wimpy platitudes, and even breaking his formality rule. He wasn't going to let this one go free, at least not at this meeting, if he could help it.

Isaac Bernstein, the diminutive Psychiatrist with the giant intellect had been sitting quietly, listening carefully, like all good Psychiatrists. His face was a mask of furrowed anxiety. Without waiting for recognition, he forged into the conversations as if he had no or little interest in the financial discussion.

"Dr. Cleary, a few minutes ago you dismissed the legal question on the basis you did not believe one would exist. I am not so certain, and I find it difficult to differentiate between what is legal and what is moral.

"I'll concede that as a profession, we may sometimes shun our responsibilities and push them onto the theologians, but I am not certain this justifies our entry into the murky field of the hereafter. Is it a moral thing for us to place your life at severe risk just for the sake of trying to prove there is life beyond the grave? Surely most people believe that or we would not have the number of churches and synagogues that we have today.

"Believe me, I am not confused about the finer points of legality versus morality. I know that all things legal are not necessarily moral, such as prostitution where it is legal, as in Nevada, but is it moral?

"Even if your experiment, Doctor, is legal, is it moral for us to deliberately take a human life in the name of science? Bernstein could see that Joe was about to interrupt, so he said, "Yes, yes, I know, you don't intend to die permanently, but my friend, we all have good intentions. These questions disturb me, Dr. Cleary. I don't know the answers."

While Isaac Bernstein was talking, the room had become very quiet. Everyone present was listening intently to each word. Isaac was stating reservations that were on the minds of many in that room. The protocol before the Committee was a radical one. It had never been done before, and even a research scientist sometimes had problems with a departure from the norm. Joe did not take Isaac's question lightly. His expressive eyes said that he was considering the question with great care.

After what was a mere moment in real time, Joe replied with a serious note in his voice. "There is a moral component, Dr. Bernstein, you're right, but I am not certain that it is the same one that you had in mind. What we are proposing is to place one human subject at risk with the potential of profound discoveries to benefit all humans. I believe the moral question is the hypocrisy of our profession on this point.

"Where are the ringing denunciations by our profession against the nearly two million human beings we kill each year in this country alone under the legal guise of abortion? Each of us in this room knows scientifically that every fetus is a living, human being. There isn't a physician here that can or will deny that fact. Where is the morality in that issue? Where are our voices of protest? Are some of our voices stilled by the fact that abortions equate to income? That is a legitimate moral question.

"I ask you, where are our moral voices against those of us who kill patients through our own incompetence and avoidable mistakes? The only reason I cannot quote a figure is because we in the profession hide that information from the public and each other, but we know it exists. We see the results of these incompetencies every day, even in *this* hospital. How moral is our conspiracy of silence? That is another legitimate question."

"Now just a minute, Dr. Cleary. You go too far," Stanton interrupted. "You are impugning every member of this Committee and the Medical School. You owe an apology to us."

"I do indeed apologize to every member of this Committee and faculty member of the Medical School if my comments seem to apply to everyone. I do not recall embellishing my statement as an all-inclusive commentary. Every member of this Committee knows exactly what I am talking about"

Joe saw that Stanton was about to break-in again, so he preempted him. "I know, I know, before you say it. We have the State Board of Medical Assurance that is supposed to be our watchdog, a place where the public can go with complaints, and the medical whistleblower can go with impunity. What happens? Very little.

"If you will permit me to continue, Bertrand Russell once said, if only jokingly, *Ethics is the art of recommending to others what they must do to get along with ourselves.* I believe medical ethics falls within that definition.

"Yes, Isaac, as I said, there is a moral question, but I believe it is a question of the morality of *not* doing this experiment, of not meeting our obligation to replace mythology of death with the facts of life."

Joe's little lecture made more than one person stop and think, maybe even squirm. There was silence when he stopped; almost an awkward pause. No one knew exactly how to respond. Joe had hit a tender spot of consciousness no one wished to expose.

Dr. Stanton, slightly flustered by the turn of events, cleared his throat and said, "The hour is late, and I have several appointments, as I'm sure most of you do. I don't think we can settle this very controversial proposal today. There are still several unanswered questions, particularly about the legal ramifications of the experiments, despite Dr. Cleary's assurances. I'm certain that Mr. Ingersoll will want this matter reviewed by our Legal Department. We could be exposing the University to some very hefty criticism . . ."

It was clear to me by the way Stanton was quickly blurting out his words that he wanted to adjourn the meeting without argument. He didn't give anyone a chance.

". . . so, we will adjourn until next Wednesday, schedules permitting, same time." With that, The Great One closed his folder, got up and walked out without another word. That was that!

The other members of the Committee looked either confused or disturbed, or perhaps a little bit of both. Stanton was able to postpone the decision, but he had been unable to stop it. Joe would have his day again.

Chapter 8

It was two days after the Human Subjects Committee meeting that Frank Picariello caught up again with Joe Cleary. They were scheduled to meet with Jim Klinger, their favorite pediatrician. Joe and Frank had been asked to operate on one of Dr. Klinger's patients, a seven-year old boy that had a heart condition with the fancy name of *Tetralogy of Fallot*. This is a not uncommon congenital cardiac anomaly in which the malformation consists of pulmonic stenosis, ventricular septa defect just below the aorta, an aorta which overrides both right and left ventricles, and hypertrophy of the right ventricle.

What all this medical technical jargon means is the boy was born with an opening between two chambers of the heart, plus some related complications. The only thing surgery could do to help him was to open up his heart and either close the lesion, if possible, or construct what is called an artificial ductus, a channel between one of the pulmonary and one of the subclavian arteries to increase the flow of blood through the lung.

With his present condition, the boy's blood was mixing between the two atrium chambers of the heart, normally separated, and therefore, some of his blood was not going through the lungs where it is normally aerated, or in other words, where oxygen replaces poisonous gases that accumulate in the blood through circulation. With a lower oxygen level, it is also possible that a particle could form in the blood, go to the brain and cause a mini-stroke.

It is uncommon to see the symptoms of *Tetralogy of Fallot* before a child is five to eight years old, although it is congenital. The earliest symptoms is normally a retardation in growth and development, sometimes coupled with easy fatigue and high blood pressure in the pulmonary arteries.

Joe would perform the surgery and had scheduled the operation for the next morning. Like most surgeons, Joe liked to see patients the day before the surgery.

The Pediatric Ward was Frank Picariello's favorite. It was colorful, bright, and decorated with Disney characters. Children are often the best of patients. They try to make the best of the situation no matter how ill they may be. Of course they are usually frightened, but they place a great deal of faith in the doctors and nurses. Sometimes the medical staff delivers on that faith, and sometimes they demonstrate they aren't the miracle workers that the public often expects.

Yes, Frank liked pediatrics, but he had to admit, it is harder to lose a child than an adult. The medical staff face death so often that most of them develop an immunity to the gut-wrenching sadness it brings to others, but not so with the children as the patients. Every time a child is lost, there are few dry eyes among the medics involved. Italian descent Frank was a sentimentalist, particularly when it came to children, but that is one of the reasons that Joe's project appealed to him. Taking the mystery out of death would help doctor and patient alike.

Jim Klinger's patient was a cute little tyke. He had the most beautiful full-head of curly blonde hair, blue eyes and a smile that had already captured the hearts of the staff on the ward. He would be a great TV model. Frank thought he would buy whatever the little boy was selling. The seven-year old was understandably thin, a normal situation for his condition.

Joe and Frank checked the child's chart. All of his vital signs appeared normal, but his red blood cell count was high. Although his growth had not been affected drastically, as in some of the more severe cases, it was obvious this little blonde angel had suffered some physical retardation. Cyanosis, a bluish or purple discoloration, was also evident on the boy's lips and his fingernail beds, a result of oxygen starvation in the blood. A little makeup and he would still make a TV star.

The chart reported that a cardiac catheterization test revealed an elevation of the right ventricular blood pressure and a relative decrease in the pulmonary arterial pressure, all symptomatic of *Tetralogy of Fallot*. There were other indications that supported the diagnosis, but it was clear this young boy needed immediate attention, and that is what Joe and Frank were going to give him.

Joe listened to the young patient's heart and lungs, checked his eyes, all the time keeping a banter going with Peter, the seven-year old's name. Joe could hear the rough systolic murmur and *thrill of pulmonic stenosis* through the stethoscope, a common sign. Joe had already studied Peter's electrocardiogram trace, the ECG, which showed a right axis deviation.

Frank also listened to the boy's heart. The poor kid must have had a dickens of a time trying to keep up with other active boys his age. With this kind of heart, he would run out of energy very quickly.

Frank examined his mouth carefully, since he would have to insert an endotracheal tube during the operation. He also felt Peter's liver for enlargement, but it seemed normal. It is physically possible to feel the liver under the ribs. He also checked Peter's peripheral arteries on the wrist, where Frank would insert catheters. This is all normal pre-op routine, but important. Doctors do not like surprises in surgery.

This was also not an unusually high-risk operation. Peter was at an optimum age for the procedure, and the loss rate was only twelve to fifteen percent. Joe and Frank had done many open-heart operations on much younger patients, and in worse condition than Peter. However, there is no such thing as minor or routine surgery.

Joe and Frank were in the room less than fifteen minutes, and all agreed, including Peter, that the operation would go as scheduled.

As the doctors were walking back towards the nurses' station, by chance Joe glanced into a patient's room whose door was open. He literally stopped in his tracks. Jim Klinger and Frank continued walking a few paces before they realized that Joe was not with them. When Frank turned around, he could see Joe looking intently into the room, his face pale.

"What is it, Joe?" he said. Joe didn't reply. It was almost as if he were somewhere else, or in a state of shock. Frank walked back to where he was looking.

In the room there was a single bed, and Frank saw what had startled Joe. Propped-up in the bed was a young girl, about twelve years old. She could have been Becky Cleary, Joe's daughter, or at least what Becky would have looked like, and just about the right age. No wonder Joe had reacted as he did.

His distraction was only momentary, and he snapped back to reality and said apologetically, "I'm sorry, for a moment I though I recognized the patient. She reminded me of someone."

Jim Klinger said, "She's a little beauty, isn't she? Her name's Pamela Parker. She is Byron Lester's patient. Sad case. She was admitted just a few days ago with advanced liver carcinoma. Her kidneys are affected too. Don't quote me, but here is a perfect case of malpractice. Her family doctor, a GP, didn't diagnose her condition because he never expected to find carcinoma of the liver in a patient so young. There's some justification for his position, but there is no bloody excuse for him not following through with tests to eliminate all doubt. He just didn't have enough knowledge to recognize the symptoms.

"When she wasn't responding, the GP finally called in a friend of his in the same medical building, an Internist, who ordered tests and recognized the problem almost immediately. They contacted Byron in Oncology. To make matters worse, she's a bleeder. That rules out a transplant. Byron isn't even certain that the liver isn't also a metastatic involvement of cancer cells from another source. I mentioned the kidneys. I'm afraid it is too late to help her from what I hear."

I should clarify what Dr. Jim Klinger meant by calling the young girl a *bleeder*, more properly referred to as *bleeding tendencies*. Strangely enough, females are not true hemophiliacs, people whose blood will not coagulate normally. Females can have bleeding tendencies, which often look much like hemophilia, a disease inherited by males through the mother.

Joe and Frank were not surprised that Pamela had bleeding tendencies, since Cirrhosis of the liver is one of the diseases associated with the condition, and this could be the root for her carcinoma.

It was obvious from Joe's eyes that he was upset by what he heard. It was also in his voice as he asked, "Is Byron certain? Can they radiate?"

"I don't know, Joe, Dr. Klinger replied. "If you're interested, you better talk to Byron. I've only been on the periphery." I could tell from Jim Klinger's voice and facial reaction that he sensed an unusual interest by Joe in the Pamela case, and assumed it was related to Joe's loss of his daughter.

As the days went by, I completely forgot the incident, but as I was later to discover, Joe didn't. However, I am getting ahead of my story.

Oh, yes, Peter's operation went well, although not without a hitch. Just after opening Peter's chest, his heart started into an arrhythmia, an irregular chaotic beating rhythm which could lead to a cardiac arrest. Joe injected lidocaine directly into the heart, and Frank started a drip of dopamine through the IV. As I said, in the medical field you must expect the unexpected.

* * * * * *

It had been a busy week in surgery for both Joe and Frank, so the days went fast and it was now Wednesday, the day for the Human Subjects Committee special meeting. The Team did not prepare additional material, assuming it would be another question and answer session.

The same Committee members were in attendance. This had become the best show in town, but only Joe, Frank and Rosie were there from the team. Joe reasoned the other members had better things to do than to sit and listen to political and legal nonsense. Feisty Rosie, however, didn't want to miss a word and insisted on being present.

Marvin Minde, the University's General Counsel was sitting along the wall, which indicated the direction the meeting would probably take. If Stanton couldn't kill the project by *crossing swords* with the team, he was going to try by *crossing "T's.*

I know, that is a terrible pun, but I am not a big booster of the legal profession, nor was Frank, since Anesthesiologists' malpractice insurance premiums are among the six or seven highest of any medical specialty. Of course Frank blamed it on lawyers, fair or not. Whoever heard of anyone blaming something wrong on themselves?

The Great One started the meeting without preliminaries and asked Marvin Minde to take the *hot seat*.

"Thank you Mr. Minde for joining us this afternoon. I presume that you had an opportunity to read the research protocol from Dr. Cleary's team."

Although Stanton said it as a statement, it was really a rhetorical question, like the one we ask people when we greet them, *Hi, how are you* without really wanting an answer. Stanton continued, although Marvin Minde looked as if he were about to answer anyway.

"Mr. Minde, the Committee would appreciate your opinion as to any possible legal question or consequence concerning the experiments detailed in the protocol. Specifically, we are concerned about the legal ramifications of putting the research subject to death. There are laws against that."

Stanton's last gratuitous remark was not lost on the Committee, nor I suspect on Joe. At least it was clear as to the tactic Stanton was employing. The Great One was never described as *subtle*.

I have never understood why a mother or father would burden a son with a name like Marvin. Don't get me wrong, there are macho guys with the name, but the only one I can think of has it as his last name, Lee Marvin.

I always got the impression of a wimp for guys with Marvin as a first name. *Wimp* is not a good description of Marvin Minde. I would guess he is about five feet ten or eleven, early forties, abundant brown, almost curly hair, and his shoulders, arms and biceps told the tale that he worked with weights. He was immaculately attired in a three-piece, dark suit that befits the status of General Counsel for a major university.

Quite a contrast to the sloppy wool shirts, corduroy pants, V-necked sweaters, and dirty yellow, raw-suede hiking boots worn by most of the liberal faculty of the University, and even some of the medical staff. Clothes may not make the man or woman, but they sure-as-hell separate the neat from the noxious.

Chapter 9

"Thank you, Dr. Stanton," Marvin Minde addressed the Committee, "and yes, I have reviewed the protocol from Dr. Cleary's team. Most unusual and challenging, not only from the obvious medical viewpoint, but also from a legal point-of-view.

"The Committee wants to know if it is legal for the Omega Project to deliberately put a subject to death, at least death as now legally defined. Through the wonderful efforts of research universities such as ours, legal death has been redefined over the years as our medical knowledge improves. Permit me to read a brief that I copied from a recent issue of a respected law journal."

Marvin picked up a paper and began to read. *"In traditional Western medical practice, death was defined as the cessation of the body's circulatory and respiratory, blood pumping and breathing, functions. With the invention of machines that provide artificial circulation and respiration that definition has ceased to be practical and has been modified to include another category of death called brain death. People can now be kept alive using such machines even when their brains have effectively died and are no longer able to control their bodily functions. Moreover, in certain medical procedures, such as open-heart surgery, individuals do not breathe or pump blood on their own. Since it would be wrong to declare as dead all persons whose circulatory or respiratory* systems are temporarily maintained by artificial means, a category that includes many patients undergoing surgery, the medical community has determined that an individual may be declared dead if brain death has occurred—that is, if the whole brain has ceased to function, or has entered what is sometimes called a persistent vegetative state. *An individual whose brain stem, the lower brain, has died, and is not able to maintain the vegetative functions of life, including respiration, circulation, and swallowing. According to the Uniform Determination of Death Act of 1980, from which most states have developed their brain death statutes, "An individual who has sustained either (1) irreversible cessation of circulatory and respiratory function, or (2) irreversible cessation of all functions of the entire brain, including the brain stem, is dead."*

Brain death becomes a crucial issue in part because of the importance of organ transplants. A brain-dead person may have organs—a heart, a liver, and lungs, for example—that could save other people's lives. For an individual to be an acceptable organ donor, he or she must be dead but still breathing and circulating blood. If a brain-dead person is maintained on artificial respiration until his or her heart fails, then these usable organs would perish. Thus, the medical category of brain death makes it possible to accomplish another goal: saving lives with organ transplants.

"Members of this Committee are aware of these points, of course, but it is important to understand the uncertainty and changing definitions of death from both the medical and legal viewpoints.

"Just as changing is the legal description of *killing*. Taking a person's life is illegal unless sanctioned by the state after due process. Killing has also been given levels of legal liability, such as the various degrees of murder, mercy killing, and killing during war. Manslaughter, another legal term for killing, is divided between involuntary and voluntary manslaughter. From a legal point, death does not enjoy a single definition.

"Another example. In recent years there has appeared a new, legal form of killing associated with the medical profession, and I know that is of paramount importance to everyone here. That is the discontinuation of life support systems on patients who have been declared to be in an irreversible coma, or brain dead. The operative word here is *irreversible*.

"Now there are movements in several states to permit the medical profession to assist in legal suicides of terminally ill patients. That controversy has even arisen here in our own Medical School. You all are aware of the sensationalism caused by the strongest advocate of assisted suicide, Dr. Jacob *Jack* Kevorkian. Perhaps more bizarre was the recent case of the physician who built a *killing machine* whereby the patient could control whether to turn on the flow of death-inducing drugs.

"Doctors and colleagues, death is a very complicated business.

* * * * * *

I feel obligated as your storyteller to add a few details about Marvin Minde. He has an authoritative voice, and many of the faculty believed that Marvin would be great in a courtroom expounding to a jury. The truth is that Marvin has little courtroom experience, and no criminal law experience. He is more at home with rules and regulations than with courtroom rhetoric. He is a good lawyer nevertheless, but not a Perry Mason. Now back to Marvin Minde whom I had interrupted with my own comments.

* * * * * *

Marvin Minde could see that some members of the Committee were looking bored, probably having heard all these preliminaries many times before. What M.D. in today's environment is not acutely aware of the law and malpractice?

He paused to take a sip of water, an old lawyer's ploy to gather one's thoughts, but before he could continue, Margaret Lowell Patterson injected herself into Marvin's presentation. She is the public member of the Committee, a community activist, and daughter of a well-known jurist, the late John Lowell, member of the State Supreme Court for twenty-two years before his death.

Margaret's husband was also an attorney, all were alumni of the University's Law School. Margaret Patterson was a staunch Catholic and supporter of the Church, which may have prompted her interruption.

"If you will excuse me, Marvin, I would like to ask Dr. Cleary a question bearing on the legal and moral issues."

Without waiting for a response, typical of Margaret, she addressed Joe. "Dr. Cleary, no matter what noble purpose is to be served, should you be put to death at your own volition, and you do not return, it would be suicide. Regardless of legalities, the moral question is clear. Suicide is against the teachings of the Church, indeed, against the tenets of most religions. Can you tell me why the University should be a party to your suicide?"

Since Marvin occupied the *hot chair*, and had the podium in a manner of speaking, Joe looked at him for his reaction. Marvin nodded to him to respond. Joe is courteous that way.

Joe replied calmly, "Mrs. Patterson, I am sorry we have not had the opportunity to meet before. Your outstanding contributions to the community and the University are well-known. I welcome your interest and question about the Omega Project." A little flattery goes a long way it has been said.

"To answer your question directly, it is not our intent to make the University a party to anyone's purposeful death. If I am unable to return from my journey into the hereafter, it will not be because I do not want to return.

"I am not being put to death out of any desire to make it permanent. If I cannot make it back, it will be an accident, not suicide."

"I understand your position, Dr. Cleary, believe me," Mrs. Patterson said pleasantly but very firmly, "but the fact still remains that you will be permitting yourself to be killed, and that is still suicide and morally wrong."

Joe replied evenly, looking directly into his interrogator's eyes, "Mrs. Patterson, Jesus Christ committed suicide"

Mrs. Patterson's reaction was one of a very astonished lady. Joe's comment startled the other Committee members as well. Before Margaret could gather her wits and say anything, which probably would have been an indignant tirade against a perceived blasphemous statement, Joe quickly explained his remarks.

"If Jesus Christ is God, as taught by many religions, then he possessed the power to come down from the cross, or to have prevented being crucified in the first place. As you said, *No matter how noble the purpose*, the fact is that Christ allowed himself to die. According to your position, that is suicide."

The atmosphere in the room turned chilly, and Joe did not make any points with Margaret. Her vote was needed to get the project approved. Marvin had the *official floor*, so he decided to jump back into the fray to prevent any further damage to Joe's case before all the facts were in. He didn't give Margaret a chance to reply.

"Getting back to the legal issues, in this State the specific code that guides us is Section 7180(a) of the Health and Safety Code. It defines death much the same as I have already read, and again the operative word is *irreversible*. There is, however, one more, what I call, *escape clause* in the State's definition. It reads, *in accordance with accepted medical practice*. In this State, that has come to mean a licensed, presiding physician, or a coroner, must sign a legal instrument called a *Death Warrant*.

"There are two essential elements that must be present for legal death to occur; a medical condition as prescribed by law, and the execution of a legal instrument by a licensed physician or coroner.

"Although there are a few rare cases reported of people dying and being legally pronounced dead and then being resuscitated, I have been unable to locate *any* case where a person has been deliberately put to death and then revived, except one unverifiable case from the state of Texas. In that case, a cattle thief was hung after conviction, but was apparently cut down too early and was found to be alive. That was in 1891, and the Supreme Court ruled that the sentence of the court had been carried out and the defendant had paid his debt to society. He went free.

"What makes the case before us of special interest from a legal point is that, as I understand, Dr. Cleary proposes that his fellow team members will physically kill a human subject, in this case Dr. Cleary himself. I use the term *kill* in the sense of the legal definition I just quoted from the statutes, and that is patently an illegal act.

"If the subject is returned to life, the death was obviously not irreversible, and no corpus delicti exists that a crime has taken place, and no warrant of death. Therefore, the legality issue would be moot. Again, the key word is *irreversible*."

* * * * * *

As the Teller of Tales, I feel obligated to inject an opinion as to the impact, so far, of Marvin's words. He hadn't made any points that presented legal barriers to the Omega Project. I suspect that Ted Stanton is probably doing a little mental fidgeting.

For once, I understood what a lawyer was talking about. Lawyers are sometimes as bad as medical doctors trying to explain something, anything, hiding behind a wall of weasel-words and jargon to demonstrate their superiority over lay persons, and sometimes, unfortunately, to hide their incompetence. I do not express that opinion openly when mingling amongst humans. *Laissez-faire* is often a good course to follow.

I could see that Marvin wanted to continue his monologue, so I will continue with the story.

* * * * * *

"The question that raises the greatest challenge is what happens if the subject is *not* resuscitated? Now we have a different set of circumstances. A deliberate imposition of permanent death introduces a third legal step. The coroner is involved no matter who signed the death warrant. The coroner is responsible to determine the legal cause of death and whether any violations of the law took place. In the case of Project Omega, I have no idea whether the coroner would step in under those circumstances and call for an inquest, since it would involve an approved research project of the University. It is doubtful he or she would require anything but a perfunctory inquest in deference to the medical staff. That is purely a personal opinion.

"The least problem would be created by a simple signing of a death warrant by a University physician, unless a surviving spouse or someone with legal standing challenged the procedure.

"I would be most uncomfortable if the coroner sought an inquest without knowing the rationale for doing so. The coroner in this county is an elected official, not an M.D. or medical professional, and there have been questions at times whether he institutes some investigations as a matter of law or politics. I am sure you are aware the University is sometimes the target of local attacks for various, often self-serving reasons."

Ted Stanton was a little anxious and wanted to weigh in, and he did.

"Mr. Minde, I share with you the concern for the University's exposure to potential problems should Dr. Cleary's experiments get out-of-hand. May I interpret your remarks to mean that you believe that the proposal is fatally flawed, from a legal standpoint, of course?"

"That is not entirely correct, Dr. Stanton. I didn't mean that it is fatally flawed. I am suggesting there is a potential for a legal problem, but that is true for almost all experiments we do at the University, even if they do not include a human subject. There is a substantial body of legal precedence for using human subjects in dangerous experiments. The Supreme Court in *Bailey versus Mandel*, also in *Kaimowitz versus the Department of Mental Hygiene,* upheld the validity of contracts to perform medical tests on human volunteers, notably prisoners, although they have come down hard on the use of non-voluntary subjects, not an issue here. The volunteers in most of these cases knew the risks involved and that death was a possibility, and in some cases a very high potential.

"As one result of these and other cases, Congress passed the National Research Act, Public Law 93-348 which puts into law the conditions under which human subjects may be used for medical experimentation.

I realize most of these facts are known to you since the University has used human subjects in many research projects. With Project Omega, we are breaking new legal ground in that we are not contending with a potential death, we are dealing with a one hundred percent certainty of death, as we know it medically, and possibly legally. Thus, the question becomes can we reverse it? If it is not reversed, the next question is whether the courts would place the experiment under the same protective blanket of *Bailey versus Mandel* as they have in cases of high-risk human experiments. The inherent problem here is if someone in good legal standing elects to file charges.

"The Coroner could file action as I said before, or it could come from the independent action of the District Attorney, or could be lodged by an independent third party of legal competence, someone recognized by the court as having a legal standing or interest in the case."

"What, Marvin, do you believe would be the outcome if the Coroner or someone else did bring charges?" That was the question asked by Vice President and Controller of the Medical School, Dick Ingersoll, not surprisingly since he had to worry about the Medical School's fiscal matters as well as its reputation.

"I hesitate to second-guess a court, any court," Marvin replied, "but as I said earlier, Dick, if the County Coroner got the case, I would anticipate embarrassment for the University, but hardly any legal action. If the subject of the research has signed the usual consent forms that we provide, I would hardly expect problems from family or professional advocacy groups like the ACLU."

Ingersoll persisted. "Do you consider it an acceptable legal risk then? Is that what you are saying?"

Marvin hesitated before answering. He assumed that Comptroller Ingersoll was trying to find someone to take the Medical School off the legal hook. Marvin wasn't prepared to accommodate him entirely, but when in doubt, he believed, it is always better to tell it straight.

"Dick, *risk* is not a legal decision. You may base your decision on legal consequences as well as other factors. I can only give you my opinion on how strong a legal case may exist if someone should legally raise an issue.

"I consider the legal risk on Project Omega no greater than with other human subject projects as I said, but with one admonition. The project is testing unchartered legal waters, and one is well-advised to proceed with prudence."

Dick Ingersoll still wanted more *hand-holding*. He looked reluctant to give up making Marvin more committal. The Legal and Finance offices had to work together, and in the end, Ingersoll did not want to push it to a point to cause friction.

"I understand your reluctance, Marvin, to predict action someone may or may not take, such as a court or the Coroner, but can you at least tell this Committee whether you see any legal barrier against Dr. Cleary beginning his project?"

Dick nailed the issue with that question, so Marvin elected to come to the point, and in so doing, probably surprised a few Committee members. He simply answered, "No."

Marvin Minde's answer was not what The Great One wanted to hear. No one else had questions, so all guests were dismissed and the Committee voted. Joe and Frank and their team won on a close five to four vote. Now all that remained was to get the full team together, kill Joe and hope to God that they could bring him back. That was a good way to put it, *Hope to God*, because if there is one, the team may come across Him somewhere along the way.

Chapter 10

When Dr. Frank Picariello left the house that fateful morning, the sun was rising, peeking from behind the mountains to the East, with tinges of red and yellow. It was a clear spring morning, the kind that lets everyone know that the earth and all its flora and fauna was giving birth to new life. Frank thought it was one of those days it felt good to be alive, and hardly the kind of day to put a friend to death.

With the Human Subjects Committee approval behind them, Joe and Frank did not waste time scheduling the activation of the project. The team had to plan dates very carefully to fit the experiments because of the heavy schedules of teaching and medical practice of team members. Now the day had arrived.

Joe called the first meeting for 8:00 AM. They met in the small conference-training room near Joe's office. Besides Joe and Frank, there was Dr. Rosamond Willett, Psychiatrist; Dr. William Ryder, a general surgeon who sometimes worked with Joe; Dr. Albert Settleman, the psychologist and test verification expert; Settleman's assistant, Adrienne Henry; Julie Diego, Circulating Nurse; Vicki Wentworth, Scrub Nurse; and Andy Gorham, the Perfusionist or Pump Technician.

In major surgery there is usually more than one scrub nurse, but since little actual surgery was involved in the tests, one was considered adequate. This is the nurse that assists the surgeon in the sterile field, while the circulating nurse assists all team members in the operating room.

Joe's intent at this meeting was to get the routine established that would be followed during the experiment. He also wanted the team to review the plans the Engineering Department had made for the *Refrigerated and Warming Dewar* (RWD) operating table essential to the experiment. Although it was already under construction after the Committee had approved the project a month ago, there was still time to make any essential changes team members might suggest.

Dr. Settleman asked Joe if he could have a console in his special room similar to the one in surgery indicating the vital signs information. He said those statistics would be important in evaluating each test. Joe agreed and made a note to pass that on to the Engineering people.

There had been numerous requests from faculty members of the Medical School to be a part of this historic team. Joe turned them all down believing it best to work with a small professional group, and to not allow the experiments to be turned into a sideshow.

Joe went over the protocol procedures he wanted to follow, then said, "We will begin the first procedure at 8:00 AM next Wednesday, which seems to be the best date for all team members.

"The first step will be for Dr. Willett to place me in a hypnotic state in the room next to OR 3." Joe used the standard initials for *Operating Room*, something the medics had in common with the Pentagon - initials.

As reported earlier and to the Humans Subjects Committee, Joe had decided early in the planning that a cessation of brain and body activity, the death state, should be induced by a gradual lowering of the body temperature until it reached the point that brain and body activity could no longer be sustained. Without getting into unnecessary medical language, the *normal* body temperature that most people know is 98.6 degrees Fahrenheit, or 37 degrees Celsius, although there are many variations of *normal* depending upon variable circumstances.

Joe figured that hypothermia induced death would eliminate any doubts of hallucinations that could be caused by drug-induced death. There are numerous reports on hypothermia used in medical procedures dating back to the Greek physician, Hippocrates, who advocated that wounded Greek soldiers be packed in snow and ice.

The downside of the process is that when the body temperature drops to somewhere around 90 to 93 degrees, body chills often develop and can become a major problem, not to mention the severe discomfort to a person at those lower temperatures. Seldom does the average person experience deep hypothermia, somewhere around 68 to 77 degrees Fahrenheit, and survive, unless successfully resuscitated as reported earlier in this story. Ice in the bloodstream can also be a problem, but with the heart-lung machine, the medical team could control the blood temperature.

To eliminate all sedative drugs from the test, but still provide protection against body reactions to the decreased temperature, Joe decided to have Dr. Willett, a Psychiatrist, hypnotize him immediately before the body-lowering procedure began. With the power of the hypnotic suggestion, Joe could be protected, in theory at least, from the side affects of a lowering body temperature.

Joe continued. "I should be ready to be placed in the RWD by 8:10 at the latest. Rosie will have hypnotized me the night before and given a posthypnotic suggestion that will permit her to place me into another trance in the morning by a simple command, speeding up the process.

"Once in the RWD, Frank, assisted by Bill Ryder, will attach me to our monitoring lines, and Andy will start the cooling. For this first experiment, we will set the RWD to reduce temperature at one degree every ten minutes. This is pure conjecture at this point since everyone reacts differently to hypothermia.

"Our best guess is there will be a cessation of life functions somewhere in the deep hypothermia stage, around seventy degrees, give or take. At that point, on this first test, and only upon orders from Frank, Andy will reverse the RWD and start the warming process exactly three minutes after Frank and Bill declare the flatline has been reached. Frank will be in charge of the timing, but I would like Rosie to back him up. Timing is critical.

"Bill had suggested that we set up a blood replacement regimen so that we could pump warm blood into my veins during the warming process. I have at least temporarily nixed that procedure because it introduces another complicating factor. I may change my mind after the first test.

"If there is some unseen emergency, Andy will have the heart-lung pump primed and ready should it be needed, but otherwise I want to keep the test clean as possible. Any questions so far?"

Bill Ryder asked, "If your heart does not begin beating naturally after you have arrived at a temperature that should normally support bodily functions, say between 80 and 90 degrees, what procedure should we use?"

"Frank and I discussed that, Bill. We believe we should wait until a somewhat arbitrary threshold of 95 degrees is reached. If then the heart has not spontaneously started, Frank should make the decision to hook me up to the pump, and you should start ordinary restart processes including electric shock, massage, and, as a last resort, you may need to make an intracardiac injection, probably Epinephrin, although I am not enthusiastic about the drug. You guys are just going to have to use your own judgement. I trust you. That is why you are on the team.

"If after an hour on the pump, and after all your heroic efforts fail, then it will be up to Frank to pull the plug. At that point, I would not say the project has failed, but that we have proven that our basic premise could not be supported with existing knowledge. That will be the end of Project Omega, not to mention the end of Dr. Joseph Raymond Cleary."

Joe's last comment failed to amuse considering the subject and circumstances. The team looked rather grim. Joe was the only one putting on a happy face.

"If there are no further questions, I will continue." Joe looked around and no one spoke. "OK then, when I am resuscitated, fully conscious and coherent, Dr. Willett will lead a debriefing session in our special recovery room. We have had that room renovated for our purposes, the one next to the OR. However, Dr. Willett will be the only one to speak directly to me. Others may ask questions, but only by writing the question on a piece of paper and giving it to Dr. Willett. I will still be under hypnosis, hopefully. Rosie is not certain that the Omega state I have been in will alter the hypnotic trance that I started with. We're exploring new ground here.

"If Rosie determines that I am still in a hypnotic state, she will conduct the debriefing without awakening me. There are some advantages to that she tells me. On the other hand, if I am no longer in a hypnotic state, then all of you may participate directly in questioning me. Is that clear?"

Frank Picariello picked up on the question. "That is clear Joe, but before we get too far along, we have a logistic problem to solve. Besides all the faculty that wanted to be on the team, we have a large number of faculty, students and some outsiders who have got wind of the project and want to attend to watch the process. Ted Stanton is one of them. We can say no to most of these people, but Stanton and some of the hierarchy? We may have to make some concessions." Trying to be amusing, Frank added, "If we sold tickets, we could pay for the project."

Joe and the others laughed, but Joe responded. "If that's true, we would need the operating amphitheater for the project. As I said earlier, under no circumstances do we want to turn this project into a three-ring circus. I'll admit, turning down the Dean of the Medical School is touchy, but I will handle that. We may end up having to make an exception for Stanton. I'll take on that problem and let you know my decision later."

Before the meeting, Frank had told Joe about Stanton's interest and Joe had responded in confidence, "Look, Frank, I don't have anything directly against Stanton, he is a good surgeon - or was. It is just that I can't stand his guts!"

Frank spoke up. "I think we should mention to the team what you and I discussed about our concern of handling reports. Not our formal medical reports to the Committee, but information releases to a curious staff or the public. I do not have much faith that information we give to the Committee will not leak out to the news media, and we could have the media parked on our doorsteps."

"Good point, Frank," Joe responded. "Yes, I did consider that situation, and I believe it wise to have Fred Johnson run interference for us. After our own team debriefing, either Frank or myself will brief Fred on the facts.

"As most of you know, Fred has been the spokesperson for the University for over ten years in his capacity as Vice President of Public Relations. He knows the ropes, and is a real pro. I suggest we refer any questions or comments to him. Does this give anyone heartburn?"

No one objected. There were no bruised egos in this group, and none of them wanted to take the time to conduct briefings and interviews.

Joe continued. "We all have ample opportunity to be amazed at the sound of our own voices in our classrooms. None of us need to invite trouble by talking to the media on our own." This reminded Frank to make a point.

"Joe didn't mention it, but speaking of classrooms reminds me that we will probably be probed by our students. We're all on our own in that situation. Handle it as you see fit, but you can be sure that whatever you say will get spread around the campus about five minutes after the class is dismissed. We are not trying to keep information from people. It is just that the nature of Project Omega lends itself to sensationalism, and we don't need that! We want to avoid an inquisitive inquisition."

"OK," Joe said, "next Wednesday it is, 8:00 AM sharp. Let's get this show on the road!"

* * * * * *

Just a side remark by the Teller of Tales. In the everyday world, people tend to speak in clichés. In telling tales, clichés are passé, but not with me. I tell my stories in the real world. In this case, Joe's reference to *show* was more factual than trite. After all, what I said earlier is still true, *Best show in town.*

Chapter 11

The team started on time. All of them were in surgical green or bright flowers on white, the latest craze, baggy shirts, baggy trousers, caps, masks and shoe covers. Designer clothes had invaded the OR. The colors were like a dash of an artist's paint against a bright white canvas as the operating room lights blazed over the sterile special operating table, the RWD. Some of the other operating rooms were painted in pastels, but not this one.

The team's OR was not one of the larger ones in the hospital, but the Omega Project did not technically fall under the heading of *major surgery* requiring a large operating staff. The special built RWD table required more space than a standard operating table, leaving minimal room for the staff, pump, monitors, oxygen tanks, and other paraphernalia common to operating rooms.

Joe had relented and invited The Great One to observe the procedure with a clear understanding that he was not to interfere with the team. Stanton was eager enough to observe that he quickly agreed to the terms.

While Rosie was preparing Joe in the adjoining room re-hypnotizing him, Andy was priming the pump, first with a saline solution and then with Joe's blood. Frank had been collecting Joe's blood over the past two weeks.

There is a little secret among medical professionals concerning blood supplies. You may hear doctors extolling in public about the safety of blood banks from contamination. The docs depend upon blood to do their jobs. When it comes to using blood for themselves, the docs are just as paranoid and scared about AIDS or hepatitis as a lay person.

Andy Gorham's pump machine looked like a large tape deck that used tape reels rather than cassettes. What looked like reels were actually three round pumps, each with a gauge and controls below. It was a relatively small machine, about four feet wide, two-and-a-half feet high, mounted on wheels, with one tall, two-inch tube on each end to hang plastic bags of blood.

Frank was giving his anesthesiologist console equipment a thorough inspection for the third time. This was not an elegant piece of equipment. The various monitors, gauges, CRTs, just like a TV, and measuring devices, together with the associated tubes and electrical lines, were all contained on a narrow, two-foot wide console standing seven feet high. With this equipment Frank could measure heart beat, brain waves, blood pressure, muscle spasms, temperature of the body as well as its various parts, pressure at the heart valves, and even the oxygen content of the blood. This latter measure was one of the most important.

Frank once had a colleague ask him during surgery for the latest stock market quotes off his console. No, Frank's console did not give that information, but since he read the Wall Street Journal every morning, he usually replied with the latest market tips. He didn't want those other medics impugning the abilities of his console!

Since Joe would be on a blood bypass to the heart-lung machine for this first trial, Frank couldn't use the blood oximeter to test for oxygen levels. The blood oximeter looked like a Band-Aid, fits on the finger, and allowed continuous monitoring of the oxygen level of the blood. Because of the bypass, Frank had to rely upon the oxygen measurement gauge on the pump, which was not too accurate, but acceptable for the team's purpose.

The team wore surgical masks, and the only thing visible on their faces were the eyes. As Frank sat on his rolling stool at the head of the operating table, he paused to look at the other eyes in the room. Andy's clear green eyes, usually his most expressive feature, were mere slits of intensity as he worked over his impressive array of valves and plastic tubes, like a scene from a science fiction movie.

Between Frank and Andy, they had worked up a routine to handle the temperature controls for the RWD. This was additional work for Andy, who normally attended to only the heart-lung pump. Even Andy's normally benign manner showed signs of anxiety to match Frank's.

The eyes above Bill Ryder's mask betrayed apprehension as he went over his tray of surgical instruments for the third time. It was a nervous habit since there was little surgery involved, other than opening Joe's arterial and Venus circuits to cool and warm the blood through Andy's machine.

The really nervous eyes were Frank's. He couldn't see his own eyes, but he could feel the tightness in his stomach. It was Frank's job to kill Joe, and I don't know how to put it more delicately. This is the first time in Frank's life that he had deliberately taken someone's life, and the first victim had to be his dearest friend. The doubts began eating away in his mind. Frank knew he could still kill the experiment by just merely saying, "No," but all that would do is delay it until Joe got a replacement.

Anesthesiologists are not an endangered species, although insurance rates may make them so, but Frank's refusal to help Joe would ruin their friendship forever. You can replace a skill, but the special relationship between people cannot be recaptured easily once it is lost. It would be like trying to put Humpty Dumpty back together again. So Frank was trapped, a prisoner of his doubts.

As Frank looked at those eyes above the masks, he thought to myself, *Here are the best trained and experienced professionals you can find, and they are all as nervous as I am, just as we were on our first surgical operation.*

It was five minutes to eight when Joe walked into the room accompanied by Dr. Rosamond Willett and Julie Diego, the Circulating Nurse. Joe did not look as if he were in a trance, but the fact he did not greet anyone and went directly to the RWD operating table was a clear sign he was under Rosie's hypnosis.

Joe was wearing one of those god-awful patient's surgical gowns, you know, the one with the opening all the way up the back that you can never get properly closed. Joe sat on the table, and Vicki Wentworth, the Scrub Nurse who assists the surgeon, untied the rear of the gown. She was also a woman in love with Joe, to which he was blind.

As Joe lay down, Vicki gently pulled the gown off as Bob Ryder pulled the table sheet up over Joe. Frank could see the yellow patch on Joe's thigh where Vicki had sterilized his skin and where the incisions would be made to insert the tubes to the femoral artery and vein. There were also yellow patches on his arms for the needles.

To clarify the story, I should say something here about Vicki since I threw in the *in love with Joe* out of the clear blue. Frank Picariello had objected when Joe had named her for the team because he and his wife, Angel, knew about Vicki's emotional attachment to Joe, who seemed oblivious to the fact. Angel and Frank's suspicions that Vicki was in love with Joe arose almost from the first time she came to dinner with him at the Picariello's house. Frank and Angel could see it in her eyes, and you know already that Frank was good at reading eyes.

Frank had told Joe that he believed Vicki was in love with him. Joe merely smiled and scoffed at the suggestion. Joe wanted Vicki on the team because she was the best, and he asked Frank that if his life depended upon the caring attention of skilled professionals who were absolutely dependable, wouldn't he prefer someone that had a personal attachment?

When Joe was strapped to the table, Frank put the blood pressure cuff on his arm, which connected directly to a readout console behind Frank. He placed an oxygen mask on Joe's face, who did not show one sign of awareness. The team had decided to use one-hundred percent oxygen throughout to clear Joe's brain of any possible residual gasses or drugs, and to increase his sensory awareness.

Frank then fitted Joe's head with the metal band with anodes that would measure his brain wave activity. This took a little calibration to get the printed chart and the CRT display in synchronization. The whole process took only about ten minutes, and as Frank was doing that, Bob Ryder assisted by Vicki Wentworth and Andy Gorman was busy getting Joe ready to hook to the pump.

Frank could already tell from his console that the super-cooled RWD, even without the transparent top in place, was starting to affect Joe's body temperature. Frank had placed a catheter hooked into a pressure tube from the radial artery into Joe's wrist. It was attached to a pressure strain gauge on Frank's console, which converts the pressure wave into electrical impulses. These electrical impulses are then translated into a wave form on his CRT, a small television-like tube. What the screen told him was Joe's blood pressure and temperature were both beginning to fall.

After all the connections were made, Andy lowered the transparent RWD cover to help lower the body temperature, similar to closing a refrigerator door.

Joe wasn't feeling any of this, as Rosie had given hypnotic suggestions that eliminated any conscious physical phenomena, including pain. Hypnosis is a remarkable phenomenon by itself, not fully understood by the medical profession, or any profession as far as that goes. If it cannot be seen, touched, or manufactured, the tendency is to send it into medical limbo, even though hypnosis has been practiced for centuries.

Frank would have preferred to use a general anesthetic on Joe than trust to hypnosis, but Joe wouldn't hear of it. His rationale was sound. He didn't want his brain clouded with chemicals or gasses that could cause interference, or later said to have induced hallucinations. He was right, of course, but Frank's professional ego was bent out of shape - slightly.

Joe's body temperature fell rapidly once the RWD lid was closed, and his blood began circulating through Andy's cooling pump. Within fifteen minutes it had fallen ten degrees, even though the RWD's temperature was falling at only one degree every ten minutes. As the temperature lowered, so did Joe's pulse rate. Everything looked normal on the instruments. The scope on the EEG, measuring brain waves, showed a decline in the peaks and a lengthening of the waves as Joe's metabolism slowed from the cold.

Within thirty minutes, his body temperature had reached 32 degrees Celsius, 84 degrees Fahrenheit, and Frank could see signs of arrhythmia, an irregular beating of the heart, a precursor to fatal ventricular fibrillation. Within a few more minutes Frank said, "Temperature 28 degrees." He believed he had said the words calmly, although he was anything but calm inside.

The EEG continued to show a slow descent from its highs and lows much like a falling stock market. That seemed like an appropriate thought because of Frank's earlier thoughts about his colleagues and the stock market. Doctors are often accused of being more interested in money than medicine. A declining stock market chart only shows losing money. Frank's chart showed losing a life.

Dead people look very dead, with a cast of gray. Cold people are more white with a slight touch of gray. It is always difficult to tell if cold people are alive. Blood pressure may not be measurable, the heart beat may be down as low as twenty. The normal pink of the fingernails, caused by capillary blood flow, is absent in the cold person. The nails will be very pale. Joe looked very cold, and the gauges confirmed the team would lose him soon.

The gauges also revealed that Joe's heart was starting into the expected ventricular fibrillation and would soon stop. Fibrillation is uncontrolled contractions of the muscle fibers of the heart with the result of losing synchronization of the heart beat and pulse. If it isn't quickly controlled, it leads to death. When this happens during open-heart surgery, cold potassium is injected directly into the heart to stop it. In most cases it is not possible to operate on a throbbing heart as mentioned before. Hence the heart-lung machine which temporarily takes over the functions. Not in this case. The extreme temperature lessened the intensity of the contractions.

"I'm getting close to a flat," Frank sounded out to no one in particular as he watched the gauges. Joe's pulse was very faint. Frank didn't need an EEG to tell him that *his* heart was pounding. The team was almost forty minutes into the procedure. Within seconds of Frank's announcement, the red light lit on his console and a buzzer sounded as he said in a not well-controlled voice, "I've got cardiac arrest." Five minutes later the EEG registered a flat line and the automatic timer turned on. Joe was dead and the search for eternity was on.

Chapter 12

As part of the Project Omega plan, the first test was designed to prove the team's ability to resuscitate the subject rather than to explore the unknown. The team began resuscitation immediately. Time was critical. Frank called to Julie Diego to start the blood flow through the heating element, and simultaneously Andy Gorham reversed the cooling lines in the RWD to heating, and the interior of the RWD began warming rapidly.

Joe's temperature was 20 degrees Celsius when the team began the reversal procedure. In ten minutes the temperature had increased five degrees. *Not bad* Frank thought. You will remember that 37 degrees Celsius, or 98.6 degrees is normal body temperature, and at this rate, normal temperature could be reached in about thirty to forty minutes. The team expected a heart beat on the ECG, or a brain wave trace on the EEG with another five to ten degrees of warming. This was a tense time.

While the team was busy around the table doing physical things to resuscitate Joe, Rosie Willett was commanding him to return to full consciousness. She was saying, "Joe, it is time to return. Return now." She kept repeating this, and it sounded like a mantra for the dead. It was the expression that Rosie and Joe had determined would be used in a posthypnotic suggestion. No one was certain whether the desire to return to physical life would be strong enough without some form of control over the process. Admittedly, the team members knew little about *any* of the process.

Joe's face still had that very white and ghostly touch of gray mentioned earlier. Nothing alarming considering the temperatures. Frank was the first to see some slight color beginning to appear on Joe's face, like a little girl's first blush he thought. He didn't know what made him think of that except for his own two little girls who were now teenagers. Joe's fingernails also began to show color which was a good sign.

"I've got a pulse," Frank cried out, a little louder and more excited than his normal operating room voice. A weak blip on the ECG was indicating a slow, but rhythmic beat. Seconds later the EEG displayed brain wave action. Frank could see in the eyes of everyone present the elation and relief.

Joe's body temperature was almost 26 degrees Celsius, still very cold, but warming quickly. Apart from Frank's outburst, the room was quiet as tension muted the team's voices. Even The Great One maintained his distance and silence as he had agreed, but even his eyes had revealed a certain amount of tenseness.

There was a slight flutter in Joe's eyelids. That told Frank more than his gauges that Joe was back into the real world. Sometimes the flutter of eyelids was the first sign seen when resuscitating a patient, but it was possible the super low temperatures delayed muscle reactions. Joe's temperature was now up to 27.8 degrees Celsius, a little over 82 degrees Fahrenheit, and the elapsed time from the start of the resuscitation was sixteen minutes.

At 33 degrees Celsius, 97.4 Fahrenheit, Frank asked Bill Ryder and Andy Gorham to take Joe off the machine. He didn't want Joe on the pump for any longer than necessary. Frank knew there were still cases of psychological dysfunction in some patients who are on heart-lung machine for extended periods. There was uncertainty in the medical field why this happened. Joe wasn't on the full pump, which as mentioned earlier, could take over both heart and lung functions. The team only used it this time to cool and warm Joe's blood.

As Joe's temperature rose, so did his consciousness. About thirty minutes after the team had begun the recovery, Joe opened his eyes, looked around, saw the smiling eyes, and blinked his eyes in response. He still had the oxygen mask on his face.

Joe Ryder was the first to speak. "Welcome back, Joe." Joe blinked back.

Frank got up from his stool behind Joe and walked around in front where Joe could see him. Frank lowered his face mask and gave Joe a thumbs-up salute. Joe blinked again. Frank told him, "We got your temperature to 35, pulse rate normal, EEG normal. You're looking good. We've removed the blood tubes, but you're still on the monitor. Let's wait until everything is normal before you try to get up. OK?" Joe nodded his agreement. Frank had forgotten completely that Joe might still be under hypnosis.

A few minutes later, after all the indicators registered normal, Frank motioned to Bill Ryder and Vicki to remove the probes and remaining tubes. They also placed compresses where the skin had been penetrated. Although Bill had made a small incision, he still had to put several stitches in the wound to close it. Frank reached over and removed Joe's oxygen mask.

Forty-two minutes after the team started the recovery, and one hour and thirty-six minutes after they had begun the experiment, Dr. Joseph Raymond Cleary had returned from the dead.

* * * * * *

Phase Two of Experiment One, Project Omega, was about to begin. This was the point where Dr. Rosamond Willett, M.D., Psychiatrist, takes over. Bill Ryder and Vicki Wentworth helped Joe sit up on the table after they had dressed his incision wound. Vicki helped him put on his hospital gown and robe. She did it with tenderness and attention. For an instant, the question Joe had asked came to Frank's mind, about who he would want to assist if his life depended upon their tender loving care. Frank now understood. Joe was right. Frank just wondered whether Joe understood how Vicki felt towards him.

Vicki and Bill Ryder helped Joe off the RWD operating table onto a gurney that had been wheeled into the OR. With the patched incision on his thigh, Bill did not want Joe to walk. Joe seemed alert, but slightly disoriented.

"Are you OK?" Frank asked.

Joe replied with a weak smile. "Sure. I'm fine. Just a little fuzzy. No problem, but I'm freezing!"

Rosie and Frank rolled him out of the OR to the room across the hall, once an office now converted to a lounge for debriefing. Frank checked Joe's pulse, temperature and heart, all normal. Dr. Settleman and Adrienne Henry would follow Rosie. None of the other team members would participate in this phase of the experiment.

Vicki poured Joe a cup of steaming hot coffee. Frank had some apprehension that Joe might get shivers from his experience, and Joe had said he was cold, but for the moment there was no sign of any after effects from his low temperature exposure. Vicki placed a blanket around him.

"Joe, is your head clear," Rosie began. I want you fully awake. Are you ready for questions, or do you want a little more time?" She was probing to see if he was fully conscious and coherent after the hypnosis.

Joe hadn't said more than a few words since he returned to conscious life. He just looked at the team and would give a little smile, or repeat the thumbs up sign. No one thought anything of it, considering what he had just been through, and that he may still be in a trance despite Rosie's incantations. Now he was concentrating on drinking his coffee as he raised himself on his elbow.

"I'm OK, Rosie. I'm awake. Let's get on with the debriefing." He sat up and swung his legs over the gurney, much to Bill Ryder's dismay.

Frank poured Joe another cup of coffee, and he thanked him. All were eager to hear what Joe had experienced, but trying not to show it. Team members were good at hiding their emotions, a professional necessity, which was particularly difficult for a real Italian like Frank, and impossible for Vicki in the case of Joe.

Joe had moved over to a comfortable, overstuffed chair with his legs supported by a built-in ottoman procured for the purpose, and the blanket wrapped tightly around him.

"Now, Joe," Rosie began, "why don't you begin by telling us what you recall. Start wherever you want. I'll turn on the recorder."

Joe took a little sip of water to clear his dried throat and then said, "The first thing you want to know is whether I experienced anything at all. The answer is, not much. The last thing I remember before the world turned black was Rosie telling me that I would not feel any pain anywhere in my body, and I vaguely remember being placed on the operating table. I could faintly hear talking as my vision seemed to slowly disappear like a round lens closing. Then everything went black.

"The next thing I remember is hearing Rosie telling me to wake up, and feeling very cold. That's it. Nothing else."

Frank and Rosie couldn't help feeling a little disappointed at Joe's brief tale, but then they had not expected much since the primary reason for this first test was to verify that the team could put Joe in the death state and successfully resuscitate him. Therefore, once Joe's vital functions stopped, they had immediately begun to bring him back. The plan was to increase the time in succeeding tests.

Joe sensed the mood and spoke. "As far as I am concerned, our first test was a one-hundred percent success. We achieved all our goals. The RWD worked perfectly, the team performed magnificently, and you all managed to bring me back from that scary threshold of death."

With a big smile on his face he said, "Team, we have successfully begun a journey into eternity."

Chapter 13

Joe's session with Rosie was short. There was also nothing for Dr. Albert Settleman or his aide, Adrienne Henry, or Frank Picariello to verify, so they remained quiet.

Dr. Ted Stanton had left the OR, and without comment went to his office since he was not going to witness the debriefing, a team's condition for his presence in the OR. He had mixed emotions. He was pleased they did not lose Joe, but another part of him was resentful at the success.

Joe's mind was in high gear now that it was cleansed of Rosie's suggestions. He had the other team members join them. After the team was settled, Joe spoke out. "We need to start the second test soon. Before you say anything, I know we have it scheduled for two weeks from now. I want to move that up before we give the naysayers a chance to weigh-in and try to stop us. I want to schedule Test 2 for the day after tomorrow. Anyone have a problem with that?"

Frank Picariello was first. "Whoa, Joe, isn't that rushing it a little bit? We aren't sure of how this first test may have acted upon you physically, and putting your body through the freezing process so soon may cause serious damage."

"Appreciate your concern, Frank, of course, but you can give me the once-over tomorrow. We all had agreed to keep our schedules open. Does anyone have a conflict on time?"

As it turned out, several team members had commitments based upon the Project's original schedule, so

Joe acquiesced, and the team was able to agree to try four days from the present, a Sunday, which normally was wide open. It meant less time with the team members' families, but medical families had become accustomed to the strange hours of their medical member. Bill Ryder did give Joe a thorough exam the next day and found him fit and not suffering from any apparent aftereffects from his extreme temperature exposure.

* * * * * *

Sunday arrived as a gloomy rainy day. The rainy season had invaded the Spring, and it had been predicted. The sky was dark and contributed to the subdued mood of the team. They were aware that today's test would increase the risk with the increased time Joe would be kept in the death state, ten minutes. The gradualism in the test time reflected the uncertainty of the team as they probed unchartered waters.

Joe sensed the concern and again reminded the team of the Swedish girl and Chicago boy who had both cheated death after a long time in the death state. The unknown is still a place that generates anxiety even in the most sophisticated of professionals.

The team went efficiently about their tasks, getting the RWD operating table and the heart-lung machine primed and ready. This time Bill Ryder elected, with Joe's approval, to reopen the incision on Joe's thigh for the pump hookup rather than create another surgical opening. No question that Joe would have a number of bruise marks where needles and probes were again inserted. This was one of the reasons the team had originally scheduled two weeks between tests.

One change was made in the process by Joe. He brought an electric blanket from home which he intended to have Vicki wrap around him when he returned from his journey. He did not want to go through the chills he had experienced the first time.

Finally, it was time for Dr. Rosamond Willett to put Joe into a hypnotic trance. This time it took only fifteen-seconds because of the previous posthypnotic suggestion. He was led into the OR, and the team repeated the first test process. Everything continued as in the first test, and a flat line was reached at 17.6° Celsius, 63.68° Fahrenheit. The timer started immediately, and the team waited, anxious as the minutes ticked off.

At exactly ten minutes, the automatic controls started the RWD warming process, and Andy began warming Joe's blood supply. As in the first test, Joe's colorization began to change as the temperature rose. The team members around the RWD operating table were showing their anxieties above their masks, none more than the eyes of Vicki Wentworth. She feared that Joe would die without ever hearing her tell him she loved him. Yet, when he was awake and going through the daily routine, she did not have the nerve to tell him. Such is the way with women in love. Men do not seem so reluctant.

Joe's temperature was now at 26° Celsius, the same temperature where he began to show life again on the first test, but this time the gauges did not show any movement. Frank was not concerned because he knew there is no constant or *norm* for this to occur. Too many variables.

When the temperature increased to 30° with still no indicator, it was not only Frank who began to show anxiety in the eyes. Seconds later Frank said, "I've got a pulse," and with those words, the eyes above the masks displayed pools of relief. Vicki's eyes were moist.

Joe's vital signs continued to improve until he was finally back into the physical world, but the expression in his eyes were not the same as when he came back from the first venture into death. Something had happened. Something very profound registered in his eyes.

Chapter 14

In the debriefing room Joe again guzzled hot coffee, but fortunately he was not chilled this time, thanks to the electric blanket that Vicki had placed around him. He was ready for Rosie and the debriefing team to begin. He was anxious this time to talk about his experience.

Rosie began, "Whenever you are ready, Joe, I'll turn on the recorder."

"You can do it now. I'm ready." Rosie switched on the machine and settled back in her own chair to give Joe full freedom to talk before he was asked questions.

"The transition happened faster than I had expected. My psyche left my body before Frank indicated a cardiac arrest. I could hear everything, unlike the first test.

"About the time Frank called the flat, I experienced the sensation that has been described by the many near-death patients, the NDEs, reported in those books and papers we read on the subject. I found myself in the corner of the OR at ceiling level looking down on the entire scene. Unlike the NDEs who were mystified by the situation, I knew exactly what was going on and took advantage to observe all the details. I knew Al Settleman had tests prepared to verify this happened.

"One thing is particularly important. I had the sense my conscious thoughts were working with extreme clarity and speed, which suggests the brain, like the body, is merely a receptacle for what we are calling the psyche. Everything I was looking at in the OR, including all the people, were in sharp focus. Not fuzzy images as often happens in dreams.

"Time seemed irrelevant, although I had a subconscious awareness of time in a manner difficult to describe. It was as if something or someone were timing my activities.

"I was totally relaxed. No fear or concern. The best analogy would be how you would feel after carrying a hundred pound weight on your shoulders all your life and suddenly having it lifted. I not only felt as light as air, I felt as though I *were* air, that I could go anywhere at just the thought. I was free of all consciousness of a material existence, no longer encumbered with a physical body. I had no sense of touch or feel, but my mind felt acutely aware, even sensing an awareness that went beyond the OR. It was an exhilarating feeling. There is absolutely no question in my mind that psychic powers are enhanced when the psyche, the mind, is released of bodily constraints. This may have some research implications.

"I can now understand how people who are deathly sick, in pain, suffering, how they must find this out-of-body state of existence to be such a relief, so wonderful, even if they do not understand what is happening. Even though I wasn't ill or in pain beforehand, there is definitely euphoria in this out-of-body state."

Joe paused long enough to drink more coffee, and the cup was promptly refilled by Adrienne Henry. That gave him an opportunity to gather his thoughts as they were racing through his brain at lightning speed. He was speaking rapidly and Rosie, Al Settleman and Adrienne were scribbling notes as fast as they could write. Joe wasn't sure why they were making such an effort at making notes since every word was being recorded. He assumed it was a part of the profession's ritual.

As before, Frank elected to listen and let the debriefing team do the questioning. Joe continued.

"I was so intrigued with what was going on in the OR, that I did not devote effort to examine other aspects of my state. I already mentioned time, but I also recall a feeling that if I concentrated, I could be anywhere I wished, instantly. That may be something else to explore the next time.

"Speaking of time, my impression was that little time had elapsed before I was aware of Frank saying, 'OK, let's bring him back.' I did have a twinge of wanting to stay longer, but there was a strong sense of responsibility to return. About then I was acutely aware of you, Rosie, telling me to come back.

Rosie asked, "What do you remember, if anything, about Al's experiments?"

"I was aware that I had experiments to perform with Al and Adrienne. The exact instant I thought about it, I instantly knew all about the experiments themselves. Even before Al wrote the words on the signboard in the OR, *'Twenty-third Psalm, Fourth Verse,* I knew that was what he would write after Frank announced a cardiac arrest. I also knew that he would hold up the sign so no one else in the room could read it. I remember thinking that Al had certainly selected an appropriate phrase from the Bible. *Yea, though I walk through the valley of the shadow of death, I will fear no evil, for thou art with me, thy rod and thy staff they comfort me.*

"The words seemed even more appropriate at the time because I had the feeling that someone was either with me or close by. It was very vague, and my concentration was then on returning to the physical world as you had commanded me.

"I thought Al and Adrienne's other test to see if I really was out-of-my-body was the best one. Adrienne used a one-handed sign language after I was officially dead, and her message that no one could see was, *Greetings Dr. Cleary from Al and Adrienne.* I have never known sign language, so I either suddenly learned it, or I was reading Adrienne's mind."

Al Settleman spoke up. "There is no question in my mind, and I am sure in Adrienne's, that you were able to read our printed sign and Adrienne's hand-signing message after you were officially *dead*. Which begs the question. If you were not dead, what were you?"

"That is exactly one of the questions we hope to solve, Al. At this point, all I can say is that I was a *presence*, neither alive or dead in the traditional medical understanding of the terms."

"The test at least proved one report we had from the NDEs," Al said." You will recall that some of them reported they had gained knowledge they had not possessed before the experience. Apparently, Joe, you also acquired a skill that you did not have before, reading sign language or reading minds. Do you believe you have retained that skill now that you are back?"

"I think so. Adrienne, try me."

Adrienne Henry had learned to sign many years ago in her work in psychology of the deaf. Her masters thesis was on the subject. This time in signing to Joe she used the conventional two-handed signing. Not only did Joe understand what she was saying, but he expertly signed back as if he had been doing so all his life. Even Joe himself was surprised.

Rosie, Frank, Al, and Adrienne looked at Joe as if they had seen a miracle performed, and maybe they had. No one had an explanation, but all in the room were aware they were a part of a phenomenon unique in medical experimentation. Despite reports by the near death experiencers as having similar gains in intellectual abilities, this was the first time to any of the team member's knowledge that the phenomenon was demonstrated under laboratory test conditions.

Rosie asked, "Besides looking down on the OR as you described, were you able to see beyond the room?"

"Well, as I said, I was above everyone, behind Frank, though I seemed to be there because it gave me the best view of the room. I felt that I could move anywhere I wished. I was aware of the clock on the wall, and that the hands were moving, but it didn't seem as if time were moving, as I also said before. It was a strange feeling, difficult to explain. I was really starting to explore my condition when it was time to go back, somewhat reluctantly I'll admit. I had a strange compulsion, the only term I can think of, to delay my return and to look around at more of my environment.

"I guess the scientist's curiosity knows no bounds, literally. I should add that when I say I was looking around, it was not like we do with our eyes. I only had to think of what I wanted to do or see and it was done."

"Was there anything unusual about your return to your body," Rosie injected.

"I already said I was reluctant to return, but when you commanded me as we agreed, I returned to my body. However, I have no recollection of any elapsed time in the process, but apparently it took about thirty minutes in real world time to get me back. I cannot explain the absence of time in my mind during the process."

Al Settleman weighed in. "You were not blood and flesh during your out-of-body experience. Do you have any idea of what physiological, or perhaps I should say, psychophysiology state your were in?"

Al had just asked the key question.

"The best I can answer, Al, considering the limitations of language, is that I was in a state resulting from the biological transformation of the human physiology by a release of concentrated energy, an energy force not known to man, but closely associated with other forms of energy that we do understand, or some form of photons, for example, electricity.

"Eastern Adepts have known of this human energy force for centuries. They called it *kundalini* in Sanskrit. That is about as close as I can come to describing it this time. Maybe we will learn more in later tests."

Rosie noted that I looked tired, so she said, "I believe we have had enough questions for this session. Maybe Joe wouldn't mind one or two more, then we call it quits for the day."

The team had agreed beforehand not to press Joe immediately after each test unless it was very important to get an immediate answer without being filtered by time. The thought then jumped into Joe's mind that Rosie wanted to ask him if he had suffered any discomfort while his body was being reduced in temperature, a question Frank also wanted to ask.

Joe volunteered, "Rosie, you and Frank need not worry about the anesthetic. It all worked well. I felt no discomfort once we started using the electric blanket after I returned."

Rosie was taken by surprise. "How in the hell did you know that I wanted to ask you that question? Can you now read minds?"

"I really don't know, Rosie. The thought just formed in my mind that is what you and Frank wanted to ask. I don't think I can read minds. I do not know what you are thinking now. This was just an anomaly."

"Maybe," Rosie responded, "but I believe we should pursue this possibility in our next test.

"OK, gang," Rosie commanded, "the session is over and Joe has got to get some rest."

A special bedroom had been set up for Joe in the hospital where he could get some sound sleep. The team did not believe it necessary after the first test where they were only testing the process. This second test was more demanding. Joe was tired now, and very willing to get normal sleep after having returned again from the *big sleep*.

Chapter 15

Frank finished lecturing to a class of first year residents, and walked down to the hospital's cafe for coffee. Joe was just entering the cafe, so he caught up with Frank.

"Hi, Frank," he said. "Join me for Java?"

"Sure. I'm free for another hour, then I have surgery. Small stuff."

They got their caffeine boost and found an empty table. With a guilty conscious, Frank had also picked up a glazed donut. Joe stuck with just the coffee; better disciplined. Joe obviously had something on his mind, Frank could sense, so let him take the lead in the conversation.

"Old Friend, I want the team to get together again by the day after tomorrow. I want to go to Test 3, a one-hour prance through the hereafter."

Joe was trying to put a little lightness into the subject, but it still shook Frank. The team was not scheduled for Test 3 for three more weeks. Another escalation of the time table.

"What's the rush, Joe? You know our plan calls for a four-week period between Phase 2 and 3. We already accelerated the first two tests. What is this one hour bit? Test 3 was planned for thirty minutes, and the team believes that is even risky. We really don't know what the situation is going to be as we increase the time, and it isn't smart to introduce unnecessary risks."

Frank didn't have much faith in his ability to persuade Joe to change. He never had in the past. Joe was quick to respond.

"I knew you would be against another acceleration and time increase, and I really do appreciate your concern. You are a good friend. Let me state it clearly. I know what can be done. I don't understand how I know, but since I returned from the last test, there is no question in my mind we can control the test for an hour. I have a reason I'll explain later.

"This time, Frank, I must concentrate on what is outside the OR environment. I must look into that other world of existence. There is where I may find some answers to our basic questions about death, about eternity.

"One other thing that I want you and the team to know, after these two tests I have absolutely no fear of death. Instead of fear, I have this strong urge to live and to seek love and knowledge. Since Linda and Becky left my life, I've really not allowed myself to love, and I've become a lousy scientist. I know that Vicki Wentworth is fond of me, and I of her, but I've even shut her out. That is not good.

"I have immersed myself with day-to-day medicine to the exclusion of everyone and everything else. I have given up the quest for new knowledge, fatal to a scientist. My life has been shallow, and I didn't fully realize it until after I died and returned.

"If anything, my dear friend, I must be careful not to enjoy the experience of dying too much, because I must return each time if science is to be served. It is not a matter of being allowed to come back, it is a matter of the will to want to return. I'm not worried now. I'm going back to that other existence the day after tomorrow, and I guarantee I will return."

* * * * * *

There are some things that even Joe could not control, like the schedules of the individual team members. Just as in the second test, there were schedule conflicts. Again, the test had to be rescheduled to a Sunday.

The preliminaries went much as before. There was heightened apprehension because of the time Joe was to be in the suspended state. Vicki was very upset when she heard the revised schedule. However, Joe finally backed off of the one hour he desired when all the team members rebelled, especially Vicki and Bill Ryder. Joe agreed to a thirty-minute compromise.

The process went like clockwork. A good team, everyone doing their job. After the timer went off at thirty minutes, the recovery began and continued normally until Joe's body temperature reached 30° Celsius, at which the team expected a heart beat. Nothing happened. At 33° Celsius, no life was visible and Frank began to worry. Joe had been gone about fifty minutes. At 37° Celsius, 98.6° Fahrenheit, normal body temperature, and still no heart beat, Frank and the other team members really started sweating.

Frank was about to tell Andy Gorham to get Joe on the full lung and heart functions of the pump when he detected a small eyelid flutter. He quickly checked the gauges on the Electrocardiogram. Nothing, and no trace on the Electroencephalograph. Nevertheless, Frank had confidence in that flutter, and within seconds there was a heartbeat, and a few seconds after that a trace appeared. Joe was on his way back, but he gave the team a real scare.

Vicki looked as if she were going to collapse when the temperature had risen to normal without any indication of life. It was probably a mistake to keep her on the team, Frank mused, but now he knew of no gentle or practical way to dismiss her. She now showed exuberance as Joe came back to life.

It took another fifteen minutes to bring Joe back far enough to take him to the debriefing room. Vicki did not want to leave his side, but Rosie told her they we could not break the team's protocol, and she could not attend the debriefing. Vicki accepted that with an expression of resignation.

This time the debriefing team was silent as Joe sat in his chair drinking the inevitable coffee. It was clear from his expression that he was either in deep thought, or deep concern. No one said anything, letting Joe take his time.

He finally set his cup down, and looked around at Rosie, Al, Adrienne and myself. Then he said in a clear voice, "My friends, today I saw God.

Chapter 16

Joe's announcement stunned the debriefing team. No one had the slightest idea of how to react. After the proverbial *pregnant minute*, Frank finally broke the silence.

"Well, Joe, if you intended to get our attention, you certainly succeeded. I can't even frame a question."

Joe smiled and picked up the conversation. "I'm sorry. I should not have started with such a dramatic statement. I just blurted it out because it was obviously the most dramatic aspect of my experience. Let me go back to the beginning.

"Everything happened normally as with Test 2. Perhaps I found myself staring down from the ceiling a little quicker than the first time, but I was keenly aware of what was happening.

"This time, however, I did not waste effort on the OR, but started thinking that I wanted to explore elsewhere. As I said from the previous test, I felt entirely capable of moving anywhere I wanted to. I decided to put that to test.

"I thought of the debriefing room, and there I was, staring down on it. Then I wanted to reach out further, so I willed myself to be in Frank's kitchen where I had spent many happy hours. Sure enough, there I was, looking down, and lo and behold, there was Angel, cooking as usual. She was the first *Angel* I had seen after dying if you will excuse the pun. I think she was preparing pasta for dinner tonight for you Frank."

Frank spoke up, "You can come home with me and have pasta with us."

"Thanks, friend, but tonight I will have a date with Vicki. She doesn't know it yet, but she soon will."

"You seem rather sure of yourself, Dr. Cleary," Frank said with humor.

"I am, *Dr.* Frank, because I can tell the future, at least some of it."

That caused the eyebrows to go up again around the room. Everyone was anxious for Joe to get on with the story. He really had their attention.

"OK, I was at Frank and Angel's house, and I said to myself, let's see what is in the other world. It was at that point I had no idea how to advance my psyche or spirit into the other world. It was as if I were in an in-between state.

"Then, in a flash of a millisecond, or whatever the measure of time is in that other world, I found myself literally propelled to the beginning of what I can only describe as a tunnel. This fits the descriptions of the NDE people. There was a very strong tug for me to go down that tunnel. My mind was still operating well, and I knew from our research that people who had gone down that tunnel often could not come back, and in most cases did not want to come back.

"I was conscious that I had a choice. Although there was that urge to go, I did not feel a compulsion. I elected to start down the tunnel, cautiously. I still felt in control.

"Movement, if I can call it that, was very rapid. I seemed to be moving at a very accelerated pace, too fast, I thought."

Rosie interrupted. "What did you see, Joe, as you were going down the tunnel?"

"I was coming to that, but perhaps this is a good time. When I first started down this oval-shaped tunnel, the sides were dark, even black. In the very far distance was what appeared to be a very small light, very bright, similar to the what we heard from other people who had near-death experiences.

"As I progressed, I had the impression that the sides of the tunnel were changing, and there were people along the sides, as if they were a part of the tunnel rather than walking down it.

"I cannot describe it accurately, a phrase you will hear often from me, but I had the sense the tunnel was something like a vortex, constantly moving, not a structure-like a huge pipeline.

"In time, if there was such a thing, I saw faces, some that looked vaguely familiar. It is difficult to describe, but when I say *seeing* something or someone, it is not quite the same as we *see* in our physical life. We have no words in the language for the sensation, so I will try to be descriptive as possible.

"That light I mentioned was a little larger as I *walked* along, and again, *walking* is a substitute word for what was happening. I felt a wonderful warmness, not in a temperature sense, but in feelings. There was a strong sense that the light was something very powerful, godlike, but that is an inadequate word to describe it. *Power*, or *energy*, seems more real to me than the word *god*. That is why I say I discovered God because I knew that what I was looking at was the ultimate power of existence. Humans understand the word *god*, even though there are vast differences in what that means.

"At that point I knew that I had to stop. It was as if there were a message from the light source that told me if I continued, there could be no turning back. It was at that point I became conscious of Rosie's voice commanding me to return. That apparently started some kind of intellectual competition between what I would call a strong desire to go to the light and an equally strong feeling of obligation to return to the physical world. Obligation won, partly because I also had the sensation the light source wanted me to return."

Joe Cleary had an expression on his face that was a mystery to team members. He seemed to beam a wave of peaceful contentment while at the same time exuding an exhilaration almost contrary to his expression. This was not the same Dr. Joseph Cleary the team had known before, and each team member seemed to come to that same conclusion as Joe told his story. Rosie jumped in.

"Joe, you mentioned the light and had used the word *god*. Is that the best term for referring to the light in the tunnel?"

"Let me answer your question this way. If I mention *Rosie* to any member of the medical school faculty, they will immediately know I am talking about Dr. Rosamond Willett. If I mention *Rosie* to anyone outside of the medical school, odds are they will search their memory for who they know by that name, and may or may not come up with someone, but not necessarily Rosamond Willett.

"The word *god* evokes the same disparities. To one person it means one thing, and to another person, something else. I can think of two names that come the closest to be a descriptive name of what I encountered, the same two I used earlier. *Power* is the first, because there is no doubt in my mind that within that light is creative and destructive power beyond the imagination of man.

"I am more comfortable with my second name, *Intelligent Energy*. The light seemed to exude knowledge and energy at the same time, another phenomenon that escapes translation into human language.

"Just the warmth from that light was enough to make me aware of things that I either did not know before or problems for which I had no previous solutions. It was an awesome experience. Since power and intelligence seem to be common terms people believe when they hear the word, *god*, I just blurted it out as another way of explaining that awesome light."

Rosie asked, "Can you give us an example of the light-inspired knowledge?"

"Sure, Rosie. I know exactly how to cure Pamela Parker."

Chapter 17

Frank knew who Joe was referring to, the adorable twelve-year old who looked like his deceased daughter, and was considered terminal from a liver carcinoma.

Rosie was vaguely familiar with the name, but Al Settleman and Adrienne Henry drew a blank, and Al was not bashful.

"Who is Pamela Parker, Joe?"

Joe explained who she was, then he added, "Her condition is complicated because she is a hemophiliac, and as you know, that is rare in a female. The cancer has probably metastasized into the kidneys. To make it even more complicated, she probably got the carcinoma from Hepatitis B and possibly C or both.

"She was born in a Chinese hospital in Beijing where her father was a senior diplomat. Pam's doctor, Byron Lester, believes that is where she acquired the Hepatitis. Very common in China.

"Lester says she probably had *hemolytic disease of the fetus,* HDFN, or as we called it in school, *erythroblastosis fetalis,* resulting in *reticulocytosis,* an attack on the red cells, and thus a *hemlytic anemia.* In Pamela, that has developed into a Cirrhosis. *Esophageal varices* may also be present, which adds to the bleeding problem.

"It is amazing the poor little girl has lived this long. She has strong resistance, but now Lester says she cannot last much longer without major intervention. It has reached a point where she would probably die on the table if surgery is attempted. She would develop massive hemorrhaging that could not be stopped."

Frank had to ask Joe. "With all those strikes against her, you still believe you can cure her?" Not surprisingly, his voice had a note of skepticism.

Joe smiled as he replied. "I didn't intend conceit, Frank, but since my journey into the other world, my brain seems to be working almost independent of my old self. Yes, I know that I can cure Pamela, and before you ask, let me tell you how.

"What we need to do is a triple transplant, both Pamela's liver, two kidneys and bone marrow from the organ donor to keep Pamela's body from rejecting the liver and kidneys. At the same time, we must give her a one-hundred percent blood transfusion, and clean out the veins and arteries to assure that nothing remains that could reinfect the blood or the liver."

Frank had to interrupt because he was on solid medical grounds where his own experience told him it could not be done. So he said to Joe, "That has never been done before, Joe. You know that. There is no way we could accomplish that and still keep her alive."

"That is exactly the point, Frank. We do not keep her alive. We bring her to the death state just as you did to me. While in that state, we can perform all the surgery necessary when her body is empty of blood. We can clean her Venus system, pump in fresh blood and bring her back to this world's life."

Frank should have been stunned at Joe's suggestion that they kill Pamela to save her, but he wasn't. In the back of his mind, he suspected that Joe would propose that solution. It led to the obvious next question. "How do you expect to get approval for such a radical treatment?"

"Trust me, Frank, that will be the easy part. I'll just tell Pamela's parents and the Human Subjects Committee that without the operation Pamela dies, permanently. With the operation she dies temporarily, and comes back cured. Take your choice. Now what do you believe they are going to say?"

* * * * * *

That is exactly what happened with the parents. The only questions during the brief session with the Human Subjects Committee were from The Great One himself, Dr. Theodore Stanton. He wanted to know how Joe could be sure there would be an organ donor available in time for the procedure, and Joe said he knew with certainty there would be one available exactly when needed. Strangely, neither Stanton or any other Committee member questioned Joe on how he could be so sure. There was something about the way he said it that mesmerized the Committee. Not one of them, even Stanton, doubted that Joe was right.

Ted Stanton's second question was to ask who would do the transplants. Joe said he had asked Dr. Peter Zambini from the University of Texas Medical School in Houston. Zambini was probably the world's most famous transplant surgeon, having studied under Denton Cooley, the transplant pioneer. Zambini liked the technical challenge, and agreed to fly to the University hospital and do the surgery at no cost. He had performed hundreds of liver and kidney transplants.

Frank was really surprised, sitting on the side of the room, to hear Stanton say, "Joe, I would really appreciate if you would permit me to assist Dr. Zambini, at no charge to the family, of course."

That was a stunner. First, he broke his own Committee protocol and called Joe by his nickname, and he made his request in a genuinely modest tone. Joe didn't seem surprised but told Stanton that he would check with Dr. Zambini, who may want his own team, but that he was very appreciative of Stanton's desire, remarking that Stanton was one of the best. Ted Stanton was not upset that he had not been asked to do the surgery because his experience with liver and kidney transplants was minimal. He was a thoracic specialist.

After the meeting and after Joe and Frank had returned to Joe's office, Frank had to ask him, "Joe, you told the Committee that you were absolutely certain that a donor would be available before Pamela dies. How can you be so sure?"

"The Intelligent Energy, the Power, or perhaps you prefer I say, *God*, said to continue to help Pamela because her time has not yet come and a donor would be there."

Joe, and the team wasted no time in preparations. He called a meeting of the team while Frank was still with him. The first time the team could assemble was that evening at 7:00 PM because they had all been busy during the day with their own schedules. They all understood the urgency of the Pamela Parker case, which Joe had invoked, so they did not grumble about the short notice.

Joe and Frank did not bother to leave the hospital. Frank called Angel and told her he would be late. She was used to those kind of calls. The two friends ate in the cafeteria, and the food was almost as bad as they feed the patients, but being Italian, Frank was picky about food. Half the time Frank did not believe Irishman Joe even knew what he was eating. It was only a necessity to him.

It was about five minutes after seven that evening the team finally assembled in their conference room. Joe explained that he wanted to schedule Pamela for surgery when Dr.

Zambini indicated he could be available, and when a second Refrigerated and Warming Dewar Operating Table, the RWD, could be built by the University's Maintenance Department.

That prompted the first question from Frank. "Why do you need a backup RWD, Joe? We haven't had any glitches."

"I'm sorry, Frank, I thought you knew. I intend to go with Pamela into the next world. She is too young to understand the process, and I need to be with her to be certain she comes back and does not elect to go towards the light."

That was another stunner. I could see the rest of the team were also shocked. Bill Ryder, the team surgeon, was the first to speak up. "Joe, you have no idea of whether you can meet with Pamela in that other world. You would be subjecting yourself to another risk. The operation may take well over two or three hours."

"That's the point, Bill. If Pamela is in the out-of-body state for that long, we may not be able to get her to return. Please believe me. I know if I am with her I can keep her from going further than the OR. There is no question in my mind that this can be done. I have a high regard for my source of surety."

"Does Pamela know about all this?" Rosie asked.

"Not yet, but her parents fully support the decision. They are at a point they would agree to almost anything, including witch doctor incantations. Anything to save their daughter, an only child."

The meeting did not finish until almost 10:00 PM, and everyone was exhausted from a long, busy day. The next day, Joe ordered the second RWD Operating Table, and pleaded with the maintenance head to expedite the construction, telling him about Pamela. He said he would have one in three days.

Next, Joe checked with Dr. Zambini, and he said he could free up his schedule and be at the University Hospital within four days by rescheduling a few nonemergency surgeries. He was going to bring several of his own team members with him, and told Joe that if any of them had a problem he would get back to Joe. Zambini said he would welcome Dr. Stanton on his team for this operation. They both knew each other.

Joe turned to Frank and said, "Zambini and I both want you as the Chief Anesthesiologist on the team, and he welcomes Rosie and our own team members to take Pamela to the suspended life state and back. Zambini and his team will concentrate on the surgery. OK?"

Frank was filled with emotion because he had been afraid that Zambini and Joe might decide to have someone else. Deep down Frank knew that Joe would not do that. Of course Frank said, "OK."

* * * * * *

The meeting with Pamela Parker was brief and emotional. Both Frank and Joe were there together with Pamela's mother and father. It was difficult for the two doctors not to show their feelings as they looked at this very sick young girl. Sick as she was, she managed a smile and showed a maturity beyond her years.

After Joe had explained the entire process to her, she said she fully understood the risk, but said she was "a little scared." When Joe told her that he would accompany her into the afterlife state, her little sick eyes lit up for an instant and she said, "Oh, Doctor Joe, that would be so nice." It was at that point Frank's eyes began to moisten and he had to turn away for a moment to regain control. Joe seemed touched also.

The two doctors kissed Pamela on the forehead and told her the operation would be done in a few days.

Back at Joe's office, he poured two cups of cold coffee from a thermos he had filled that morning. Both he and Frank sat silent for a minute as they drank and collected their thoughts. Joe was first to break the silence.

"Well, Frank, it all boils down to this. In a few days we will know whether I have been having delusions or really have tasted the afterlife. If I have been delusional, we will kill Pamela Parker. Even though she is practically dead, clinically, it would still be tragic.

"On the other hand, if I was not delusional, and we are successful in saving Pamela, do you realize what will happen next?"

Frank thought this was probably a rhetorical question, but he answered anyway. "No, I really haven't thought that far. What did you have in mind?"

"My dear friend, not only will Pamela's life be changed forever, but so will our lives. Already news of the surgery has leaked out in the Medical School and possibly out of the University. The demands for seats in the operating theater would make you believe we had a winning Las Vegas show. It won't be long before the press smells a story and we will be deluged. Much as I hate the idea, I probably should alert the University's Public Relations Department to be prepared and to keep the vultures away from us. Let PR handle the press. Do you agree?

"Absolutely, Joe. Glad you thought of it. This could rapidly degenerate into the proverbial sideshow. Do you want to handle it, or would you like me to talk to PR?"

"You do it, Frank. You are co-chair of the project, and besides, you have that Italian charm that all good PR people admire."

There was more than a little lighthearted sarcasm in Joe's comment, but that is the way Frank and Joe had always been. What neither of them knew was just how much of a public relations avalanche they would cause.

Chapter 18

Because of the unique nature of the surgery on Pamela Parker, and the appearance of world famous Dr. Peter Zambini, the Medical School's main operating amphitheater was used. It was packed. There were seats for what would normally be a hundred medical students plus ceiling mounted video cameras and screens. The cameras would display the surgery in detail through the University's television network to a number of auditoriums. For this surgery, another five hundred medical students and faculty would observe the operation. All observers could see the operation as if they were looking down on the operating table, much like Joe had described when he was in his out-of-body state.

As Joe had predicted, there were leaks to the press. He had talked to Fred Johnson, the University's Vice President for Public Relations. He agreed that this surgery should not be open to the press or public for two important reasons. First, Pamela's parents considered it an invasion of their daughter's privacy, and second, the possibility of adverse publicity should complications develop. Johnson was a realist, however, and knew that someone in such a large audience - and probably more than one - would leak information to the press. Johnson also put a strict security hold on all video material, and issued a ban on cameras

Before beginning the actual surgery, Albert Settleman, Phd, agreed to brief the attending faculty and students on the procedure that would be used, the hypnosis anesthetic, details about the RWD Operating Table and its use for inducing a cessation of life functions through hypothermia.

For the operation on Pamela Parker, Dr. Settleman had no role to play and that is why he was selected to do the briefing. He knew there would be many questions on the audiences minds, but wisely advised that no questions would be taken until after the surgery.

Pamela was easy for Rosie to hypnotize. At her age, she was susceptible to suggestion, particularly from such a warm person as our Rosie. She hypnotized Pamela first because to hypnotize Joe required only a simple posthypnotic suggestion command Rosie had used on him previously.

The hypnosis was timed to the point where the two RWD's were ready at the correct temperatures to begin the procedure, slightly cooler than body temperature.

Although Dr. Frank Picariello was in overall charge of the double process, Dr. Peter Zambini was clearly in charge of the transplant surgery. The organs were brought into the OR, having been flown in only hours before from the East where they had been removed from an eighteen year old boy involved in an automobile accident several days before, and who was brain dead while his body continued to function.

His parents had made the decision to *pull the plug* on keeping his body operating, and quickly agreed to donate the organs to the twelve year old Pamela. She was Number One on the recipient priority list, and both the young man and Pamela were a blood match suitable for transplant. Joe had again been proven right when he said there would be organs available for Pamela. His abilities got stranger by the day.

The timing was to get Joe into the flatline condition before Pamela was brought to that state. Joe wanted to be waiting for Pamela. He insisted that he knew this would happen, and at this point, no one seemed to question Joe's source of supreme confidence. Everyone felt he was right. Strange for so many scientific minds to accept such a revolutionary idea without doubts. If there were doubts, no one gave life to them.

It took twenty-one minutes for Joe to reach a flatline on the EEG. Unlike the first test, Joe found himself looking down on the OR within two minutes of reaching the flatline. He saw in exquisite detail the progress of Pamela Parkers descent in temperature. Frank and Andy Gorham had started the process ten minutes before, and Pamela's body temperature had already decreased by seven degrees.

Her temperature dropped off sharply at that point, and because of her weakened condition, cardiac arrest and brain wave flatline were achieved almost simultaneously when her body temperature reached 75.6 degrees Fahrenheit. It had taken seventeen minutes. Pamela Parker was dead.

* * * * * *

Dr. Peter Zambini had added his partner, Dr. Lester Rosenfeld to the team, a renowned transplant surgeon in his own right. Rosenfeld had performed over 800 kidney transplants.

Zambini had gained his fame by his special techniques which reduced the normally four-hour transplantation time for a liver to a two-and-a-half hour or less procedure. Since a kidney transplant was also involved as well as bone marrow, the availability of Dr. Rosenfeld increased the chances of success.

Dr. Zambini and his team started immediately. The team was well-aware this was a race against time. Zambini signaled for Dr. Rosenfeld to begin draining Pamela's blood.

The main obstacle to the transplants was the crowded working area presented to the two surgeons. Only superb, experienced surgeons could handle the extreme conditions. They considered it imperative to keep the surgery within a two to three hour maximum time.

With the blood removed, Anesthesiologist Frank Picariello released nitrous oxide into Pamela's cardiovascular and lymphatic systems through the mask on her face. Although known as *laughing gas*, it is best known as a mild anesthetic, which would be helpful to relieve pain from the incisions when Pamela awakened. In this case, however, its prime use was to cleanse the two primary systems that carried blood before fresh blood was introduced.

Once that was completed, Dr. Zambini made the first incision in Pamela's emaciated body. He worked quickly and deftly. It was soon apparent that the draining of the blood helped immeasurably in reaching and removing the diseased organs.

When the surgery began, a member of Zambini's surgical team prepared the donor organs for insertion. Each one required anastomoses, medically linked by many sutures and reconnections of blood vessels and organ structures inside the little body of Pamela Parker.

There was no turning back.

* * * * * *

"Oh, Doctor Cleary, I can see you." Pamela's psyche had materialized to Joe as he observed from his position high in the OR.

"Welcome, Pamela, to a new world just as I told you. You OK?"

"I feel wonderful. No pain. My brain does not feel fuzzy as before. I can see so clearly, just like you said it would be, but it does seem silly being up here on the ceiling."

"Now Pamela, just as I had told you, it is important that you and I talk and watch what is going on down below us. You will remember that I had said you might get a strong desire to explore your new surroundings, but you must not wander from the OR.

"Although time has no meaning to you and me, the doctors below us will be working on your body for three to four hours. During that time, I will explain what they are doing, and you can ask any questions. The important thing is to keep in touch with me until Dr. Willett tells us it is OK to return. Is that all right with you?"

"Gee, yes, Doctor Cleary. I feel so good. I hope I feel this way when I go back to my body."

"You will, Pamela, you will."

* * * * * *

The surgery took only three hours and seventeen minutes to perform, due primarily to two skilled transplant surgeons working together. It also helped that their patient's blood had been removed.

Dr. Bill Ryder had been recruited to do the close up of the abdominal opening, and he did the finest stitch work of his career. Pamela's scar would be thin and almost invisible.

Frank finally gave the signal to Andy Gorham to transfer five quarts of new blood back into the lifeless body on the table. Pamela's mother had donated bone marrow for transfusion, and it had been added to the whole blood now entering the body.

Andy and Frank had also adjusted the RWD to begin the warming process. Rosie would begin her posthypnotic incantations for Pamela to return when her body temperature reached sixty-five degrees Fahrenheit, 18.33 degrees Celsius.

Joe had insisted that he not return until it was clear that Pamela was able to be resuscitated. Therefore, Rosie would not begin her hypnotic plea to Joe until Pamela's heart began to beat and her brain trace showed activity.

Strangely, Joe did not hear Rosie telling Pamela to return, and was taken partly by surprise when Pamela's psyche was no longer in his view. Looking down on the scene below, Joe knew that all was going well.

It would be at least twenty minutes before Pamela's body was up to normal temperature, so Joe decided to take advantage of his freedom and explore deeper into the chasm of eternity *in the next room.*

Chapter 19

Pamela Parker came back to the physical world without any indications of a problem. All signs pointed to a successful transplant, but the full success would not be known for at least a few days to be sure all the *plumbing* was operating as designed.

When she opened her eyes on the operating table, they were at first not focussed, but soon she was looking at the anxious faces of Doctors Zambini, Rosenfeld, Ryder and Picariello. She rewarded all of them with a smile, even though they all assumed she was still under the influence of Dr. Willett's magical hypnotic trance.

Pamela was disengaged from the tubing except a saline drip into her blood stream that contained a mild anesthetic against pain from the surgery. She was wrapped in a special electric blanket, thanks to Joe, and wheeled off to her own private hospital room.

Instead of retreating successfully from the operating battlefield, Doctors Zambini and Rosenfeld turned together with the Omega Team to the task of bringing Joe back to the world of the living. The visiting surgeons stayed in the background, their work completed. Dr. Rosamond Willett stepped up front and began her imploring chant for Joe to come home.

By the time that Joe's body temperature had risen to 82° Fahrenheit, almost 28° Celsius, with still no sign of life, the team did not panic, but were a little anxious. The same thing had happened the last time.

However, when the temperature gauge registered normal body temperature and still no heart beat or brain wave, the team was visibly concerned. Vicki Wentworth's eyes showed panic. Joe wasn't answering his psychic telephone.

Frank had already ordered Andy to start the heart-lung machine when Joe's temperature had risen to nearly 90 degrees. For the moment Frank was all doctor and not thinking about Joe other than as a patient.

A small blip on the Electroencephalograph appeared after seven minutes, which seemed like an eternity to the team, a rather ominous use of the word. Soon the ECG registered a blip and a heart trace began. There was a twitch of the eyes. Joe was coming back after all.

Frank told Andy to withdraw the machine support, but to keep oxygen flowing one hundred percent. Vicki placed an electric blanket over Joe and everyone waited.

Joe's eyes popped full open quickly, unlike previous tests where his eyes blinked their way into the world. This time, Joe's eyes looked deep in color and very intense. No one was certain what this meant, if anything.

"Welcome back, Joe," Frank greeted. "We wish you would not take extended side trips. You had us all concerned."

Joe looked at Frank, who could see no emotion in Joe's eyes. Joe turned his head and looked at Vicki. His eyes seemed to warm a little, and then he looked straight up at the ceiling with his eyes expressionless.

Rosie said, "Let's get him to the debriefing room." He was quickly moved on a gurney to the special nearby room. Because this was not a part of the test protocol, no formal debriefing was scheduled, so the whole team flowed into the room. Drs. Zambini and Rosenfeld and their team members retired to the dressing room as their job was over. Pamela Parker's regular Pediatrician, Dr. Byron Lester, and surgeon Dr. Bill Ryder, took over the care of the patient.

The Public Relations guru, Fred Johnson, had the job of whisking the visiting medical team to the airport so they could quickly return home to Texas. Their time was heavily booked into the future, giving credence to the marketing mantra that *if you have a good product, the customers will flock to your door.* Flock they did.

In the debriefing room, Rosie gave the posthypnotic command to Joe to awaken from his trance. In response, and surprising all, he sat up on the edge of the gurney and told Rosie, "Thanks, Rosie, but I came out of the hypnosis by myself, a new found skill. I also believe I can put myself back into a trance, but I will not try it now."

"Do you want to talk about the experience now, Joe, or have a rest first?" Rosie asked.

"Let's do it later if you don't mind. I need to think about it awhile before discussions. I'll tell you this, I learned things that no human has known before, and I need to gather my thoughts."

"Of course, Joe. Whenever you are up to it. Are you up to going home now?"

Vicki Wentworth jumped into the discussion, "I'll take him home. He probably should not be driving right now, and it is on my way."

Everyone knew Vicki had that protective instinct towards Joe. Even Joe had come to realize that she was in love with him, but he had been evasive because of the tests and the strong possibility that something could go wrong.
Nevertheless, the idea of having Vicki with him at this time appealed to him, and he agreed.

* * * * * *

It was late afternoon when Joe and Vicki pulled into Joe's long driveway. In the house, Vicki quickly went to the kitchen to pour a glass of wine. She also checked the refrigerator to see what food was available as she wanted to cook dinner. Joe was in no condition to cook for himself or go out. It was obvious that she was at home in Joe's house.

Joe did not argue, but removed his coat and shoes, unbuttoned his shirt and relaxed on his favorite recliner. Vicki brought him a glass of his favorite Cabernet Sauvignon and some cheese she found. Then she sat on the couch with her shoes off and her legs tucked up on the couch, her favorite position. She said nothing, waiting for Joe to take the lead.

After a few sips of the rich red wine, and a period of total silence, Joe finally spoke.

"Vicki, what I found today no one is going to believe. It will change centuries-old beliefs, and rock the foundation of almost every religion that has ever existed. I am not sure what to do."

Vicki promptly responded with, "You know that you have the right to do or say nothing. Our team would understand."

"Oh, I agree, I could clam up, and the team would respect my decision, but the University and the public would clamor for an explanation.

"I could also lie and say nothing happened, but you know me well enough to know that is not an option."

"Would you like to try it out on me, Joe? I am a good listener."

"Yes, you are, and I trust you and your opinion more than anyone else, you know that."

"I believe you do, Joe, but you are a little *standoffish*. You always seem to hesitate for us to get too involved."

"Vicki, I realize I have been resisting my impulses, and it has only been recently that I allowed my emotions to finally take over. I believe I am in love with you, but as long as these tests are taking place, I admittedly put my emotional brakes on. If I do not make it back from one of my ventures into the unknown, I do not want to leave you in the same emotional hell that I was in after losing Linda and Becky."

"Joe, I am already emotionally involved as you call it. If you are really in love with me as you say, that is what matters. I can wait if that is what you want."

"Vicki, it isn't exactly what I want, but I am afraid that if we become more involved, I will lose my incentive to see Project Omega through to a logical conclusion."

"What conclusion is that? It is not even clear in our Omega plan."

"You're right, it isn't clear, but then it is rather difficult to define the unknown. I do have my own objective. I want to reach a scientifically supported conclusion about the death state, its meaning and how it fits into the pattern of human existence. After today's experience with Pamela and my side trip further down the tunnel of eternity, I know that I am close to the ultimate answer.

"Today I learned the answers to two of the three questions probably asked by every human from the beginning of time. Where did we come from, and what is our purpose?"

Vicki was stunned at this information. She asked, "And what is the third question?"

Joe looked at her with steady eyes as he replied, "Where are we going?"

Chapter 20

After Joe told Vicki what he had discovered in his latest psychic escape from his body, she was visibly shaken. Joe could understand that. What Joe had discovered was not easily explained in human language, and did challenge human traditions and previous knowledge. Still, he was now faced with the obligation to convey this information to the Project Omega Team regardless of what their reaction might be. There was always that chance they will believe the experiences have affected Joe's sanity, and perhaps they would be right. Joe was having difficulty sorting it all out himself. He was sure about one thing, however, and that is the urgent need to again travel to the next world for that final answer to the question, *where are we going?*

The Omega Team gathered the next morning at 10:00 AM. Joe had invited Fred Johnson, the PR Vice President, since he would have to handle the onslaught of the media. After the usual greeting chitchat, Joe began telling them about his experience in his latest afterlife venture.

"There is no way that I can describe all that happened to me," Joe began, "for the simple reason as I have repeated many times, there are no human words to describe events that no human had previously experienced, and then was able to relate. Our language has not kept pace with knowledge, so I will attempt to relate what happened in the best, if not totally accurate way that I can.

"The first and most important finding for the team is that it is possible to take a person to a state where the heart and brain are no longer operating, keep them in that state for some time, the total time still not scientifically determined, and then bring them back to a normal physiological state, apparently without harm. During that period when the patient is technically dead by current medical and legal definitions, major surgery can be performed.

"At this point we cannot state without equivocation that therapeutic hypothermia used to such an extreme is a method that should be applied routinely. For instance, it is not established that patients can always be resuscitated. Our proof so far has been under controlled laboratory conditions.

"You have all heard me describe my impressions about the long tunnel, which resembles a horizontal, transparent vortex with an intensely bright light at the distant end, and the impression I had of people, many people, being a part of the walls of the vortex. As I walked towards the light - and again, the term *walking* is not accurate - I had the sense of communicating with my wife, Linda, and daughter, Becky, but no one in the tunnel. The messages I was receiving were incoherent. I wanted to continue moving towards the light.

"The further I progressed, the more clear my thoughts. I felt as if my mind was filling with new knowledge, again using terms that we can comprehend.

"Finally, I reached a point where there was a sudden upload of data that flooded my mind. At that instant, I knew the purpose of humanity, yes, even the entire universe. I felt no elation but more a feeling of calm satisfaction and understanding.

"I can see in your faces that you want me to immediately reveal that secret that has challenged people from the beginning, and I will, but first I must relate a little history or my revelation will be meaningless."

Joe paused for a sip of coffee. He was doing all the talking, but no one on the team seemed eager to jump in. They were mesmerized.

"I'll try to make this brief," Joe continued. "Most civilized societies recognize that all nature seems to have a defined purpose, although we have not yet discovered the extent nor the purpose of everything. That is essential to all other beliefs.

"We also accept that nature has a defined food chain, hierarchal in nature. Lower forms are consumed by higher forms. The strong feed upon the weak. Without that chain, there could be no life.

"Sitting on top of that food chain is Homo sapiens, supposedly the most advanced and strongest. Have you ever had anyone ask, who does Homo sapiens feed? Are we the end of the food chain? Does the universe exist only for the benefit of Homo sapiens? Is ours the only universe?

"What I have discovered is that the answer is *no* to all those questions. To explain that, I am again forced to remind us of what we do know about Homo sapiens that is relevant here.

"Talking to a group of medics, I hardly need to remind you that the human body is an electrochemical machine, and that it generates measurable electrical impulses, the electroencephalograph is the best example.

"The main point is, however, that the one electrical impulse we know little about is the electrical aura surrounding the body. Medical speculation backed by research is meager at best what this aura represents. Some objects in our universe have mass, like protons, while other objects such as photons, the constituent of light, possess only energy. The aura is pure energy, but it is also the essence of human life. Some would call it the *soul*, but that has the wrong connotation, and you will see why. For the moment, stay with me.

"When my heart and lung functions ceased operating, in other words, medical death, it was that aura, that body energy, that went to the ceiling and was looking down on the operating room.

"The so-called *light at the end of the tunnel*, is pure energy, Intelligent Energy of a magnitude impossible to describe. That Intelligent Energy is capable of all things. It is also the very top of the food chain for all worlds. It is the ultimate Power.

"The human aura, the pure energy that is the essence of all humanity, that part of me that wandered down the tunnel, is food for that Power, and that is the end of the food chain and the purpose of human existence."

Chapter 21

In Dr. Rosamond Willett's twenty-one years as a practicing Psychiatrist, she had heard some unusual stories. What she just heard from Joe had to take first prize. *My God*, she thought, *he is babbling about some electrical power or energy, or something that he makes sound like he has met God.*

Rosie had known Joe for most of her professional career, and she did not remember him ever acting strangely, or making ludicrous statements. He always seemed like the consummate professional, reserved but always likable and possessed an intelligence greater than most of his peers.

All she could surmise was that the experiments causing hypothermia and long absence of heart and lung functions, had affected his brain in some strange way. If that was so, he was certainly telling his story in a rational manner as far as she could tell.

There was also the possibility that Joe was telling the team something so profound that their rational brains were unable to comprehend, or perhaps the word *accept* is better.

Rosie had to ask him, "Joe, are you telling us that this Power you saw, this *light at the end of the tunnel*, is the last in the food chain? Is God?"

Joe looked at Rosie with eyes that she could not comprehend. They were deep pools, bottomless pits of mystery. They revealed nothing, but gave her a feeling of warmth and trust. Now, even Rosie was having difficulty finding the right words. Rosie the Psychiatrist lost for words? Something strange, indeed, was happening.

"Rosie," Joe began, "the term *god* has many meanings to people on earth, many interpretations. It is a religious term, not a biological word.

"However, to answer your question, the Intelligent Energy, or the Power I met, is not describable in human terms, but most humans would understand it best by calling that phenomenon by a term they do comprehend, *God*.

"I will not use that word in my descriptions of what I encountered because it is misleading and will be interpreted in people's minds according to their religious beliefs. That could cause real differences in reactions. I do not wish to cause unnecessary confusion.

"To the point of your question. The Power I met was the source of all creation, and of the many universes, all life forms, the reason that everything exists."

Frank Picariello jumped into the conversation. He asked, "Joe, you said human energy is merged with the Power, in other words like a fuel feeding a furnace or an engine. Is that on target?"

Joe smiled at his closest friend and replied, "You never cease to amaze me, Frank. You always were a head above the crowd. Your analogy is about as close as I could come to explaining the total process. Yes, human energy feeds the Power. I don't want to confuse you, but there are other forms of energy that originate from other sources than earth to feed the Power, and they are not necessarily humans as we understand the term."

Frank came back quickly with another question. "If we are fuel for the Power, as you say, then what does that mean? Are we consumed like fuel and that is the end? Sounds more like feeding fuel to the fires of Hell than Heaven."

Joe laughed. "Since I have known you from the time we were young boys, I can understand your concern about Hell," Joe quipped, and everyone smiled, "but being a good little Boy Scout, I cannot tell a lie. The answer, Frank, which you will be happy to hear, is there is no Hell of fire and brimstone.

"When the human psyche or energy merges with the Power, you become a part of that existence. The Power represents the energy of everyone who has ever existed whose psyche or energy force is able to reach the end of the tunnel and merge with the Power.

"Not everyone on earth or elsewhere, when they die, has sufficient energy to reach the end of the tunnel and the Power, or as you call the Power, *God*. Those that cannot reach the Power become a part of the long tunnel, forever watching the psyches of others pass by as they are caught in the vortex of eternity. That is Hell."

Frank continued to press his friend. "Can you be sure of all this, Joe, or is this a figment of your imagination from the unusual condition in which you were placed? If this story leaks out, and no doubt it will, you know the withering criticism and skepticism that will follow. What you are telling us is impossible to prove."

"As are almost all religious beliefs, Frank, but people still want to believe. It is called faith. You do, however, touch upon an important element of our research, however that needs to be addressed.

"We need some physical evidence that life extends beyond what we now call death."

Bill Riley spoke up next. "Why do we have to prove anything more than we have already, or I should say you have proved?"

"Because we haven't proved anything more than the fact someone can be legally and medically dead and still be resuscitated. Hell, Bill, we already knew that.

"If possible," Joe continued, "we should attempt to prove that medically, death of the body is the normal progressive process of life. We should attempt to prove that life has a meaning beyond the grave. Religions have been making this point since the beginning of life on earth, but it was more of an instinctive belief, blind faith more than belief backed by fact. I want it to be a fact based upon medical science."

Frank asked, "Are you suggesting, Joe, that we still need another answer?"

"Not so much an answer, Frank, as some form of proof."

"Proof of what, Joe?"

"Eternity, Frank, eternity."

* * * * * *

Talking about discovering eternity is heady stuff, and for the most part, the team was listening to Joe with incomprehension, and a growing sense of alarm. They had not bargained for a medical research leading to God, or at least what they understood to be God. Joe was trying to lead them away from that understanding, but humans have difficulty discarding long-held beliefs.

Team members were not ready to let Joe off the hook. Al Settleman picked up on the *proof* statement that Joe had just exclaimed.

"Adrienne and I are thoroughly convinced by our tests that you were indeed in some form of out-of-body situation, and we do not believe we will have any problem convincing a skeptical public of that assertion. At his point, however, we haven't the foggiest how we can devise tests to prove eternity. There are times we would be happy to prove there will be a tomorrow!"

That brought a smile on everyone's face, even Joe's, who responded.

"Al, even with my newfound knowledge, and my certainty there will be a tomorrow, I can't prove it either!"

In a more serious vein, Al asked, "Then if you cannot prove tomorrow, how will you be able to prove eternity?"

"Have no idea, Al, but then, how many past scientific searches knew in advance of the outcome? Like the guy said, *I don't know what it looks like, but when I see it I'll know it.* I guess that answers your question, too."

Rosie finally got to her other question. "You mentioned that we humans are among others that provide what you called psychic fuel for the Power, what you also called *Intelligent Energy*. Does that mean there are other humans or creatures in our universe that also provide this energy?"

"I was afraid someone would ask that question, Rosie. I don't mind the question, it is that I have taxed everyone's credulity with what I have already said. However, I will not evade your question. I will answer it the best as I can with my new knowledge.

"You said *Our universe*. The truth is there are millions, trillions, countless universes beyond human understanding. Within each of these universes are life forms that also have energy that ultimately feed the Power, the Intelligent Energy of eternity.

"These universes, and our own, are like gardens of energy. They are collectively the *gardens of the God*, and the Intelligent Energy Force is the *Gardener*."

Chapter 22

Doctors Cleary and Picariello invited public relations guru, Fred Johnson, to their team's debriefing. As a guest, he chose to remain silent and listen. What he heard started his stomach churning. In the public relations business, particularly in a medical environment, stomach churning is an occupational hazard. It is only medically serious when the churning turns to ulcers, which they may well do as a result of what Fred Johnson just heard.

Johnson immediately recognized that once the press corps and TV anchors got ahold of the story, there would be a 24/7 buzz that would occupy him and his staff full time, and then some.

The first thing Fred decided he had to do was to attempt to control leaks. He had already briefed the team and everyone else involved in the Pamela Parker procedure to refer any media enquiries to his office. Fortunately, Fred knew the team did not have any *prima donnas*, but he had no control over the visiting medics, Doctors Zambini and Rosenfeld. Fred asked their cooperation before they had left, and they at least promised to refer enquiries to him.

Fred's major concern of a leak source was Dr. Theodore Stanton, a well-known publicity hound. Fred knew that he would have to keep his eyes and ears open for that potential.

Attempting to control the flow of information is a tricky business. The public has a right to know how their tax dollars are being spent, and although the University is a well-endowed private school, the specialist schools and faculty, and students, accept Federal dollars for various and sundry purposes. Many Americans believe they have a right to know about significant happenings in major institutions of learning, private or public. Vice President Johnson's job was to assure that information released was accurate, complete, and safeguarded personal privacy. That was the challenge.

Despite all his precautions, Fred Johnson always assumed there would be a leak, and therefore, he prepared for it. The PR office seldom discovered sources of leaks since many of them were inadvertent. That was what happened about Project Omega, except it was discovered that the source was not Ted Stanton as expected, but the University's Maintenance Department that had built the RWD Operating Tables. One of the engineers of the device was discussing it with a colleague at a trade convention. The conversation was heard by a reporter of a small tabloid covering the convention, and from that source, it was picked up by the Associated Press. There were no details, but tabloid headlines like, "Miracle Child Brought Back From The Dead" was enough to stimulate a PR uproar.

Then the phones began to ring.

* * * * * *

The University Public Relations office received literally thousands of calls from news media from all over the world. There was no way they could respond to so many in a standard press conference. Doctors Cleary and Picariello and Fred Johnson decided the best response would be to release the team's report. The only problem was the team report had not yet been written.

The three decided to write an abbreviated version of what would eventually become the team's report, but in layperson's language. As the chief PR voice for the University, Fred had the task of writing the press release based upon dictated notes from Doctors Cleary and Picariello.

Johnson's staff reviewed the many questions from the press and TV, and attempted to incorporate answers into the press release. Experience told Fred this would not satisfy the paparazzi who were tenacious in their pursuit of *celebrities, causes and catastrophes.* In the trade, the paparazzi were called *Three C Cowboys*, always trying to *rope-in* their victims.

"The PR office attempted to organize the thousands of questions received by grouping duplicates and preparing a master list of questions which were then given to team members to answer. Joe Cleary and Frank Picariello reviewed a sample of the questions and the team's responses.

This first question was the most frequently asked. *Although I can understand the rationale used in Pamela Parker's case to use the extreme hypothermia method for anesthesia, what is the value of this technique to other surgical procedures?'*

Dr. Picariello was asked to answer this one since he was the anesthesiologist.

Frank dictated to his recorder, *Lowering of body temperature is commonly used in surgery and has been for centuries. It lowers the metabolism and thus decreases the amount of oxygen needed for the brain.*

However, Project Omega was not primarily focused on developing a new anesthesia technique, but on basic research into the death state condition of the human body.

Within our lifetime, the definition of death has changed dramatically as the news media is aware. Even the definition of life is subject to controversy, so I will not delve into technical matters, but just say that as scientists, we are dedicated to finding truth in all matters that we pursue. In this instance, we seek the truth in death.

As to the question, I believe there will be further instances where the use of hypothermia may be warranted in surgical procedures on a limited basis.

Fred Johnson thought Frank Picariello answered that question quite well.

The next question was submitted by Barney Fitzsimmons of the Miami Gazette and 231 other journalists. They asked, *How can we be certain that Dr. Cleary was in an out-of-body state? Isn't it possible he was in a dream state rather than a death state? The same question can also be applied to Pamela Parker.*

That was clearly a question for Dr. Cleary, so Fred Johnson asked him to dictate a reply. Like Frank, Joe dictated for later transcription. *A sure way would be for one of the reporters to accompany me on my next out-of-body trip. I suspect that is not what the questioners had in mind.*

The research brief that you have been provided includes a summary of Dr. Albert Settleman's process for 'keeping the team honest,' so to speak. Dr. Settleman's full report will be available from the Medical School within two weeks . Unless you believe Dr. Settleman and his staff are dishonest, it would be hard to dispute the evidence they gathered that I and Pamela Parker were, indeed, observing the operation from the ceiling in the operating room.

The next question was typical of the press' *show me* attitude about science and scientific breakthroughs. Cynthia Callahan from the Allied Press Association and 214 other journalists wanted to know, *"Why haven't we seen Pamela Parker since the surgery? It has been over three weeks, and certainly she should have recovered enough by now to be interviewed or seen, unless there was a problem."*

Joe Cleary had been waiting for this one and dictated the answer.

Everyone who asked this question has every right to be suspicious. I will spare you all the clichés, and instead tell you that Ms. Parker's parents believe she will heal better and faster if she is not subjected to the stress of public appearances. They believe their daughter's health and privacy is of more importance than the public's right to know. They have said she will make an appearance soon. In the meantime, she has recovered very well, and all the previous symptoms from the cancer and deteriorating body functions have disappeared. She is in remarkably good health.

There were many similar questions, but those were the three that Fred Johnson had highlighted as examples. There was one other question Fred had brought to Joe's attention, but did not ask him for an answer. The question had nothing to do with medicine, but Fred knew it had the potential of causing more headaches than all the other questions combined.

It was the proverbial *bomb shell*. The question came from a reporter on a local newspaper, and no one on the team or in Fred's office had any idea how the reporter had received the information. *Dr. Cleary was heard to say that during a recent out-of-body experience, he was propelled down a tunnel with a light at the end, and that the light was God. My question is, can you confirm that statement, and what did Dr. Cleary mean that he "found" God?*

Chapter 23

When Fred passed the question about Joe's *God* statement, Joe was surprised. Questions were supposed to be about the Pamela Parker case. Nothing was mentioned to the public about the earlier Project Omega tests, so how did this information get leaked?

Joe could not think of anyone on the team who would purposely leak confidential information. The report of the second experiment was still in draft form, yet, by the reporter's question there was no doubt there was a leak.

Then it hit Joe like a brick as to the source of the leak, himself! He remembered that after that third out-of-body experience, he had gone to the cafeteria with Frank. That was after the team debriefing, the one where Joe had said *I had found God.*

Frank and Joe had both been hungry, and both had surgery scheduled the next morning. The tables in the cafeteria were close to each other so that conversations could be easily overheard by the occupants of the next table. Most of the staff were immune to the problem and talked freely in the cafeteria.

At the table next to Joe and Frank were three medical students, two females and a male. They were in animated, cheerful conversation as they ate, and the two doctors paid no attention to them. As Joe thought back, he recalled that the male student appeared to take an interest in Joe and Frank's conversation, although it was nothing overt, and Joe thought nothing of it at the time. Joe wasn't certain the male student was the source of the leak, but that was the only source he could identify as a possibility.

The source was not as important as the University's response to the questions from the press once they heard the information.

Fred Johnson and Joe knew the news media would sensationalize the subject, and the University would be deluged by people from all over the world. Joe decided to call Fred and discuss the problem.

Joe asked Fred, "What do you want me to do with the question?"

It was obvious by his answer that Fred had also been thinking about the problem. "We don't have too many choices, Joe. If we ignore it, the reporter, Michelle Ambrose, is going to make a big deal out of our refusal, and would probably say things like, 'What are they trying to hide?' The Administration would not be happy with that."

Joe said, "The Administration is not going to be happy no matter what we do or say. This story is gathering a life of its own, and the Chancellor is one conservative cat. So, what are our other alternatives?"

"We could play it straight and tell them exactly what you experienced, although that alternative does not excite me too much. It would open too many *cans-of-worms*.

"Of course, we could lie a little, or as an alternative follow the old adage, *Don't ever lie, just don't go around blabbing the truth.*"

Joe smiled at Fred's attempt at humor, but they still lacked a good course of action. He suggested, "Why don't we follow that other old adage, W*hen all else fails, try the truth?*"

"I admire your morals, Joe, but not your PR savvy. The truth will cause a monumental fire storm. The Chancellor will have our butts in his office within five minutes after the story breaks. We need to be more creative."

"I caused the problem, I'll fix the problem," Joe offered bravely, although not too convincingly. "As the Great Bard said, *truth will out*. If there are any repercussions, I'll take them. I'm a big boy, Fred, and frankly, I am more interested in our Project than I am the Chancellor's feelings.

"The publicity should be a boost for the University," Joe continued, "as the world will know we are on the leading edge of medical research. The University will get a million dollars worth of free publicity. I am convinced, my friend, that truth is *our* out."

"OK, Joe, write it like you want it. That is what we will go with."

* * * * ** *

It took two days to write and rewrite the answer to reporter Michelle Ambrose's question. This is what Joe said:

During an out-of-body experience within the Project Omega research, I found myself at what appeared to be the beginning of a vortex-shaped tunnel. In the distance I could see a bright light. At that moment, I realized that I could still return to my earthly body upon my will to do so. I could also hear my controller, Dr. Rosamond Willett, giving me the command to return. I had been placed under a hypnotic trance by Dr. Willett as part of the transition to what our research team calls the Omega state.

I was also aware that I could move towards the light with some safety, and that I could still return to human life if I so chose. All of this was sensed in a manner difficult to describe in human language.

I continued towards the light for what seemed like a short distance, although the word 'distance' has no meaning in this strange tunnel, the place my psyche was located.

As I came closer to the light, I was aware that my knowledge level was increasing. By that I mean, thoughts began forming about subjects that previously I knew little or nothing about. The only way I can describe it is like getting four years of college absorbed within a few seconds.

For instance, I began to realize that the light was not a light in our human understanding. It is more like a field of energy or power or both, and I don't know how to describe it better. It is not unlike the situation when lost tribes were found in the jungles of the Amazon. Never having seen any modern society, everything was new to them, and their language had no words for what they were seeing.

My next realization was that I was looking upon the universal power that could create, and indeed, did create all the universes and all matter.

As I thought the question. I was told that living creatures on earth and on all the planets in the trillions of universes existed to provide sources of energy to fuel the power I was beholding. I believe I called these universes the Gardens of the God.

Not knowing how to accurately explain this incredible phenomenon of powerful energy, I had inadvertently used a word understood by humans, God.

That was a poor choice of words, as the Power I sensed was not the God of Christians, Jews, Muslims or any other religion. This was a Power that transcends all religious beliefs.

About the time of these revelations, I sensed that I could go no closer to the light or I would be absorbed and unable to return to the mortal world. It was at this point I willed myself to return.

I learned much more, but that will take time to digest. I will write a more detailed report within the next several months. In the meantime, there are at least two questions to which I do not have the answer and which I may still seek answers during our Project Omega.
The first of these questions is, 'Does our psyche remain individualistic, or is it absorbed and lost in something bigger? In other words, do I remain Joe Cleary for eternity, or something else?
The second question, 'Is there an eternity?' Project Omega has not decided whether to pursue the answers to these questions, but should the Omega team elect to continue, we will keep the press informed."

After reviewing this statement with Project Omega team members, Joe gave it to Fred Johnson. He read it carefully, and when he finished he looked at Joe with an expression of a man who had just learned he had been condemned to death, a rather interesting thought considering the subject.

"You realize don't you, Joe, this piece of paper challenges thousands of years of religious beliefs? Your soul will be condemned to Hell by every religious zealot on the globe. Do you really want that?"

Joe had to smile at what he considered Fred's exaggerations, although he fully understood his concern. Fred was a smart guy, and he could handle the problem. Joe responded, "Whenever a new theory or discovery is made, there are always skeptics, and the subject does not have to involve religion. Skeptics are good because they help weed out the charlatans from the serious researchers. No, Fred, we should welcome criticism and questions. It keeps us on our toes and honest."

The next day Fred sent Michelle Ambrose a letter with Joe's abbreviated reply to her question. The following day, Ambrose's paper, true to tabloid form, announced in big headlines, *Researcher Claims To Have Found The Meaning Of Life*.

Although the headline was provocative, it was close to the truth.

Chapter 24

Fred Johnson was not entirely correct. Instead of his predicted five minutes, it was thirty minutes after the paper hit the street that Fred and Joe Cleary were summoned to the Chancellor's office.

"Congratulations," the Chancellor began. "You two have managed to ruin my day twice within a week. That's a record. In my twenty-two years at this University, I don't believe anyone has managed to do that before.

"My phone began ringing even before I called you. Here we go again. We are faced with the question on how to handle the press, and I am certain, an outraged clergy will follow quickly, then comes an upset citizenry whose understanding of life and death has just been challenged. Another press release is not going to solve anything!"

The Chancellor was not prone to colloquial speech and provocative rhetoric, but when he got excited it seems that all his graces vanished. He could cuss with the best of them.

"Before the Board fires my butt, here is what we have to do. We need a plan. I don't worry about the press. They are always going for the most bizarre part of every story. The clergy are the ones that we must satisfy and quickly. Some of our largest donors are very devout people and they may think twice about giving to what they perceive as a University of Kooks! So what would you propose, Fred?"

Fred Johnson was no amateur, and he had anticipated the Chancellor's wrath. He responded.

"You're right. We will have to deal with the clergy first. I suggest we invite senior clergy from each of the major religions to attend a lecture by Joe's team on their findings, giving emphasis to the medical research aspects and attempting to play down the religious aspects. This should be followed by a question and answer period."

"What do you think of that, Joe?" the Chancellor asked.

Joe said, "That may be the way to go. I have no problem with it, and I doubt the team would object. I cannot promise that our report and answers to questions will squelch the intense interest. It may create an even bigger demand for information."

The Chancellor asked, "Where would you get money for such a meeting? The University has nothing in the budget for this, and I doubt the Board would approve funds unless there was some way we could get donations or the participants to pay to attend."

"If we invite specific clergy, they are going to expect reimbursement for expense. If we open the meeting to any member of the clergy who wishes to attend, we open ourselves to being inundated with every fringe religious nut who wants to make a statement. We lose control."

"I've got a few bucks in my PR budget that I could use, but not enough," Fred volunteered.

Joe jumped in. "I can come up with some money from the Omega Project and my own personal assets."

The Chancellor added, "I guess I could put my hands on a small amount. Why don't you two make up a budget of expenses and how much you can raise between the two of you. I will try to make up the difference. Fair enough?"

The money was raised and the meeting scheduled for one month from the current date. After much debate, the team, Chancellor and his VP of Public Relations then decided to invite the senior cleric in the major religions in the United States, defining *major* as any religious sect within the United States with a congregation of at least one percent of the population. The University Library research staff came up with a list which provided Fred Johnson with a guide.

It was clear that Christians at 70% of the population would need more than one representative, so Fred Johnson, Joe Cleary and Frank Picariello opted to invite the heads of the major Christian church groups, and one each from the other religious groups. In all, they invited twenty-two ministers, prelates, rabbi and other senior religious notaries. No list was made public, nonetheless, when the word leaked out about the conference and the list, the Public Relations and Chancellor's offices were deluged with requests for invitations and outraged indignations for not being included, including a scathing letter from the International Allied Atheists Association.

The Atheists letterhead showed organizations in fifty-three countries as partners, although their actual numbers were not known. It was believed to be about 16% in the United States population. Joe said, "What the hell, Project Omega is about medicine, not religion, so invite the head of the Atheist organization. His or her reaction to the team's findings might be interesting."

Of course the press corps screamed at being excluded.

* * * * * *

The conclave convened promptly at 9:00 AM on Thursday, June 17, an unusually warm and muggy day. The air conditioning was a welcome relief in the Medical School's lecture hall that had been chosen instead of a more formal and larger conference room or theater. The team's psychiatrist, Dr. Rosie Willett, thought the lecture hall environment would set the right tone for an academic research project and not some PR stunt.

The Chancellor himself elected to do the welcoming of the group, which included such luminaries as the Apostolic Papal Nuncio to the United States, the Presiding Bishop of the Episcopalian Church of America and the outspoken New York Rabbi, Mordecai Schwartz. The United States does not have a Chief Rabbi as found in some countries.

The Atheists chose a controversial female member of Congress from Oregon. She occasionally made the news by her relentless fight to change the National motto, *In God We Trust*.

The other invited clergy were considered serious scholars and experts in their particular religions.

In his opening remarks, the Chancellor decided not to recognize anyone special for fear of offending others. He was accustomed to making politically correct talks, and warned the team to be careful not to offend any of the attendees. He was *preaching to the choir* since the medical members of the team were acutely aware of how missteps could result in lawsuits in a litigious society.

Dr. Theodore Stanton, *The Great One*, Dean of the Medical School, was introduced, and told the audience of the genesis of Project Omega, giving himself as much credit as possible. Members of the team cringed at his words, but kept their faces relatively neutral.

After fifteen minutes, Stanton finally introduced Joseph Raymond Cleary, M.D., Professor of Medicine, and Project Omega's chief researcher and the human subject.

Joe gave a brief report of the team's methodology and purpose with emphasis on the medical implications of the research, finishing his introduction with the words, "We are seeking medical facts, not religious truths."

He then went on to report in detail the results of each out-of-body experiences, much as he had written for the news media. It was at this point he chose his words with special care.

"Before you ask questions, please consider the three most salient points. First, my out-of-body experience is scientifically proven, not a subject of conjecture.

"Second, what I witnessed during my out-of-body experience beyond the operating room may not have been scientifically proven by Dr. Albert Settleman and his experiments, but what will come as a complete surprise to my team, except for Dr. Rosamond Willett, is that we *did* perform a secret test for a journey beyond the operating room."

This piece of news caused a surprised expression on the faces of Frank Picariello and other team members, and a quizzical look by Fred Johnson. The clerics in the audience were on the edge of their seats. Joe continued.

"After my first venture into the unknown, I had discussed the problem of the verification tests with Dr. Settleman and Adrienne Henry. They were helpful and promised to give it some thought. In the meantime, I mentioned the weakness in the testing methods to Dr. Willett, whom you have already met. She thought about it for a few moments and then offered her suggestion.

"She said, 'Why don't I reveal some information that no one else in the world of the living knows except me? I can write it down, have it notarized and sealed in an envelope and have it stored in a lockbox by a trustee at the bank.'"

What Joe didn't reveal to his audience was his initial skepticism. He had responded to Rosie's idea by saying, "But Rosie, that is similar to what Al and Audrey are doing."

Rosie jumped right back at him, "You didn't let me finish. I know something that my grandmother told me when I was a young girl, and she made me swear that I would not reveal it to anyone while she was still alive. After she died, I decided by then there was no reason to tell anyone, and so to this day I have not revealed Grandmother's secret.

"What I am suggesting, Joe, based upon what you have told us, is that you can ask my grandmother what it was she told me, and if you get an answer, the right answer, who can dispute your journey beyond the OR?"

"Now wait, Rosie," Joe quickly said, "I have no idea whether I can contact your grandmother or anyone else for that matter. I merely said that I had the impression I was surrounded by family and friends without actual conversation with them. I would hate to have our experiment's legitimacy based upon such a relatively flimsy test."

"But Joe, how else can you prove your experiences beyond what you observed from the ceiling in the OR? I doubt you will find anyone who will want to go with you just to prove your point."

"You are certainly right there," he smiled.

Although Joe did not reveal all of this conversation with Rosie to his audience, he had revealed enough to garner their curiosity, waiting for the revelation that would anchor his claim of out-of-body-experience beyond the operating room.

Joe continued to his audience. "On my most recent visit to the beyond, I called out to Rosie's paternal grandmother for whom she was named, Rosamond Willett, not knowing what would transpire. Almost instantly I heard a voice that said, *Hello, Joe. It has been years since I saw Rosamond, but I know what you are here for.*

Joe explained, "I want all of you to realize that what I am telling you is not similar to a conversation between humans, but in the ethereal land of the beyond, it was more like an exchange of thoughts.

"Grandma Willett said, *Rosamond wants me to tell you the secret that only she and I know in order for your clerical audience to believe you are in this state between mortal life and eternal life. I will tell you the secret, Joe, but it will not satisfy your critics. Take comfort in that you are making great medical strides. As for Rosamond's and my secret, it is that her father, Benjamin, Sr., was not my biological son, but had been adopted from an unwed mother when he was born.*

Joe told his audience, "I did not tell Dr. Willett before this meeting that I had communicated with her grandmother." Turning to Rosie, Joe asked, "Is that correct, Dr. Willett?"

Rosie was not surprised. Joe had told her he would reveal the secret at the meeting and not before. She responded, "You are right, Dr. Cleary, you did not tell me before now whether you had been able to contact my grandmother and whether she revealed her secret. There is no question in my mind that you did meet her in an afterlife situation since she died over twenty-three years ago. That *was* the secret she told me."

There was stirring and exchanges among members of the audience. Finally, Archbishop Pietro Allegro, Apostolic Nuncio to the United States, a tall, almost ascetic-looking man with a full head of brilliant white hair, capped by his violet skull cap, called a *pileolus,* rose from his chair to be recognized. He wore a black, well-tailored suit with an ecclesiastical vest and collar. Joe immediately recognized him by name and asked him to speak.

"Thank you Dr. Cleary, and my thanks to the University for organizing this conclave. I accept without question, Dr. Cleary, that you have experienced a true revolutionary jaunt into the spiritual realm and have been able to come back and tell us about it. The proof is indisputable.

"I have one question. Did you meet God as it has been reported in the news media?"

Joe gave himself a moment to think about the question before answering. "Your Eminence, that was a question asked by one of my team members. I will give you the same answer.

"The word *god* has a definite connotation to most humans. As you know better than I, it is a religious term with different meanings among different sects. Therefore, I cannot answer your question with a simple *yes* or *no*. Rather, I will report the truth of what I know without embellishing it with personal opinion.

"I know there is a power that is Master of this and all other universes.

"I know that I can describe this power only in terms that humans can understand. I have described this power to my team members as being a powerful source of Intelligent Energy, as I explained to this audience.

I know this Intelligent Energy requires reinforcement, or you might say, *fuel*, to continue its existence.

I know that humans in this universe provide a source of intelligent energy to feed the primary source of power. In other words, humans provide fuel by their own energy psyche.

"Now whether, Your Eminence, you wish to attach the name *God* to the ultimate Intelligent Energy Force, or even admit its existence, is a matter best left to you and your Church. I am merely a messenger, and hardly an angelic one at that."

Chapter 25

The psychological effect of Joe's revelations upon the audience of clerics was an interesting study by itself.

The professional psychiatric side of Dr. Rosamond Willett saw the emotional struggles going on in the minds of many of these clerics as their whole world of beliefs was being challenged by a medical doctor based on what most of them considered to be wild dreams or hallucinations at best, and a possible conspiracy at worst. It seemed impossible for a few to believe that all Joe was telling them was the truth as he saw it. He had not convinced everyone. Archbishop Allegro had another comment.

"Dr. Cleary, I recently read Leo Tolstoy's book *The Kingdom of God Is Within You*, and that reminded me of what he had said in 1901 when he was excommunicated by the Russian Orthodox Church because of his views. He said at the time, *I believe in God, whom I understand as a Spirit, as Love, as the Source of all. I believe He is in me and I in Him.* It seems that Tolstoy had come to the same conclusions as you have described with your encounter with your Intelligent Energy Force. I find that interesting .Tolstoy did not die to arrive at that conclusion."

Joe replied, "I, too, have read Tolstoy's book. Long before that gifted writer penned a word, an ancient unknown wrote the *Book of Genesis*. In Chapter 1, Verse 27 he wrote, *So God created man in his own image.* You can understand,

Archbishop, there is no inconsistency between what I experienced and what many others have believed, taught, sensed, or even perhaps experienced in the same manner that I have. We all agree."

"Your analogies are quite to the point. If I may be permitted a follow-on question," the Archbishop said, and continued when Joe nodded. "How can you be so sure that your Intelligent Energy Force, the *light at the end of the tunnel* is indeed the final link in the so-called food chain? Might not there be other dimensions, other tunnels, other lights at their ends?"

It was obvious that Joe was giving that question deep thought. He finally responded. "The answer is *no*, I cannot be certain, although my mind tells me it is so. I believe the ultimate truth of what I observed will only be found when the psyche merges with the Intelligent Energy Force. As I said, it was my instinct that said that was a final step and no turning back if I made that transition.

"For purposes of our medical research, those questions became secondary as we had already proved to our satisfaction that the psyche survives the body, and that mortal death is only a continuation of mortal life."

Although Joe was encouraged by the Archbishop's words, he also sensed there was some hesitancy or question in the cleric's voice and expression.

No sooner had Archbishop Allegro begun to sit down than another member of the audience stood up and began talking without any introduction.

"Dr. Cleary, what you are speaking is pure blasphemy! We have thousands of years of learned teachings from God's own words through his Son, Jesus Christ. The Bible has warned us of false prophets, and I ask you, other than the games you played with Dr. Settleman of your team, exactly what proof have you that the Bible is not the word of God?"

Frank said to himself, hoping that Joe could read his mind, *Oh, boy! We got a pot stirrer. Stay calm, Joe. Let the guy hang on his words for a while before you answer. Don't lose your cool.*

I believe Joe did read Frank's mind. He did not immediately respond, but looked down in thought. He finally said, "Reverend Peters, I take your concern seriously."

Now how did Joe know this guy's name? How did he know the previous cleric for that matter? They are not wearing nametags, and there is no seating plan.

Joe continued his answer. "The Holy Bible was not our medical research plan, nor was it our task to prove or disprove its source. If our scientific findings conflict with teachings of your Church, the fault is not necessarily in the results of the research, but a reconciliation between what is scientifically proven and that which is a matter of faith. A conflict between science and religious philosophy is hardly a new subject.

"What I reported about my journeys does not *prima facie* disagree with your dogma. Our research merely adds to a better understanding of your faith. It is similar to the impact upon your faith if you suddenly discovered the Ten Commandments had not been carved in stone but engraved on a piece of solid aluminum? That would hardly change your faith in the Commandments, now would it?

"Even in the Bible you find well-known incidents of people dying and then resuscitated after days in the death state. Recall the story of Lazarus who had been dead four days and came back to life. The Bible reports that Jesus Christ said at the time, *I am the resurrection and the life. He who believes in me will live, even though he dies; and whoever lives and believes in me will never die.*

"According to the Bible, Jesus Christ was dead for three days and then came back to the living. So, Reverend Peters, it seems to me that the Bible was way ahead of our team in describing out-of-body experiences and resuscitation. What our team has done is to provide scientific confirmation that it is possible for the body to die and then be resuscitated within some finite, but undetermined amount of time. One of our research objectives is to explore what is that amount of time.

"In other words, Reverend Peters, our research supports the Biblical tales, not confronts them."

Good answer, Joe, Rosie thought, but kept her opinion to herself. Already, more hands were in the air.

"Bishop Helen Hagemann, you have a question?" Joe asked. Rosie and other team members were again mystified by Joe's apparent knowledge of all attendee's names. Rosie made a mental note to ask Joe about that.

Episcopalian Hagemann asked, "You keep reminding us that your research was medical and not theological, yet what you describe touches on the faith of every religion represented in this room . . ."

Before she could continue, the atheist member of the audience, Congresswoman Janet Ogle, spoke out, "Does not touch my faith!" That elicited a small laughter from the clerics.

"My apologies to the lady," the Reverend Dr. Hagemann responded, "What Dr. Cleary described touches upon the faith of *most* people in the room, so my question is, Doctor, do you believe your research confirms that the soul does indeed survive the death of the body?"

Joe was again thoughtful before replying. "Bishop Hagemann, we are again confronted with a term that has a religious connotation. The soul is called different names in different cultures - spirit, psyche, inner self, inner being, life force, vital force, individuality, makeup, subconscious, *anima, pneuma*, and in Hinduism, it is called *Atman*. My team settled on the accepted term in the medical field of Psychology, the psyche.

"In answer to your question, yes, the psyche, or soul if you prefer, does survive the cessation of life's body functions. As I remarked, the psyche is an energy force by itself, something that has been known to the medical profession for many years. It can be observed as an aura around the body. The difference is that we can now state with more assuredness the function of the aura."

"If I may, Dr. Cleary, I would like to ask a follow-up question," Bishop Hagemann continued. Without waiting for a response she asked, "If the soul does indeed survive the body, and then as you say, melds into the massive, I believe you called *Intelligent Energy*, then does the soul remain as an individual, or is it consumed like in a fire and loses all of its original human identity?"

Joe responded immediately, "Now that is a profound question, Bishop Hagemann, and I will tell you directly that I do not have the answer. Your analogy to *fire* is interesting, and I can assure you the Intelligent Energy Force is not fire. Isn't it in the Bible that Hell is the place of fire and brimstone?" Joe got a little laugh from that exchange.

"It is my sense that to know the answer, I would have to become a part of that Intelligent Energy Force, *the light at the end of the tunnel*. I also have an understanding that if I allow my psyche to merge that I would not be able to return to my mortal body. So, in that respect - and this is a pure guess - the psyche loses freedom of choice, but not its individualism. That is evident because of my experience in talking to Grandma Willett. Her psyche, or soul, whatever, had definitely melded with the Intelligent Energy Force, but she was still Grandma Willett."

That brought a few more smiles although Joe had not intended it to be humorous.

"The Reverend Michael DeHaven has his hand up." Again Joe knew the name of the participant. That still puzzled Rosie. As a Psychiatrist, it was clear to her that Joe had developed extrasensory perception. She made a mental note to discuss this psychic ability with him.

"What is your question, Dr. DeHaven?" Joe asked.

"I apologize in advance if my subject causes any anguish, Dr. Cleary, but it seems important to ask."

Joe immediately assured the minister not to be concerned.

"Thank you, Dr. Cleary. When you were describing your out-of-body experience contact with Dr. Willett's grandmother, you did not mention any contact with your own wife and daughter who had been tragically taken from you not too long ago. That seems a little unusual. I would think you would be more anxious for that contact than with Dr. Willett's grandmother. Is there some reason?"

Frank would have told Joe to respond that it was a personal matter that he did not wish to discuss, but no, Joe had his own way.

"You are absolutely correct, Reverend, that my personal desire was to contact my family. The Project Team even discussed that as a possibility. As a group we decided that to permit personal feelings to influence the project would be counterproductive to the objectivity of our research. I totally agreed with that conclusion, thus it was imperative that I follow the teams guidelines for the research.

"That isn't the whole story, however. When I was on my Grandma Willett search I had the distinct and strong feeling of the presence of my wife and daughter. They were encouraging me to continue with the test and they fully understood the need to keep the process professional.

"All of this, you must understand Reverend DeHaven was not communicated in a manner that you and I and other humans communicate.

"At the same time, those thoughts did not have any effect upon my quest to get an answer from Grandma Willett. I know my wife and daughter are safe, waiting for me, and that brings much comfort.

"I hope that answers your question."

"It does, and quite well, thank you, Dr. Cleary."

Joe moved on.

"Your Eminence Metropolitan Nicholas, you have a question?" Joe asked as he saw a hand raised no higher than the shoulder of the cleric.

In a voice soft and restrained, the Greek Orthodox Bishop said, "Tell me, Dr. Cleary, did you find a Heaven and a Hell?"

"Metropolitan Nicholas, those are two more religious terms, not medical. They also demand definition. I have no idea of whether there is a Biblical Heaven or a Biblical Hell. What I can do is relate my experience as I traveled down the tunnel towards the light.

"As I reported earlier, I was aware of people, or I should say, psyches or souls that seemed to be part of the tunnel itself. Their numbers were legion. I had the sense they were in great disarray, and trapped in a warp of eternal time. They were not a happy bunch.

"As I wondered about their plight, an answer came into my thoughts explaining that each person's psyche is an energy source like electricity here on earth. We have positive and negative charges, and we all know that opposites attract.

"This new source of information told me that the human psyche accumulates both negative and positive energy over a lifetime, and when the psyche moves on into the hereafter, and begins the journey down the tunnel of eternity, it is either attracted or repelled by what I have termed the Intelligent Energy Force.

"Perhaps, Your Eminence, that is the essence of Heaven and Hell. Either the psyche is trapped in the tunnel for eternity, watching other souls merge with the Intelligent Energy Force, a Hell of sorts, or it merges with the Intelligent Energy force in what you would call Heaven. Those two terms never entered my conscious mind during my journey."

"That is an amazing answer, Dr. Cleary," the Greek priest replied. It is very different from the *fire and brimstone* you mentioned, and that we all have been taught. Then again, and unlike your claim, those who taught us our religious beliefs have never made a roundtrip excursion to the hereafter. You have given us room for thought.

"If as you say, Dr. Cleary, the psyche or soul accumulates energy strength throughout a lifetime, what happens to the souls of newborn babies who die? They have had no time to accumulate energy to make their way to God, I mean the 'Intelligent Energy' of your experiments?"

"Metropolitan, the souls of newborns are pure, unadulterated energy that has had no time to accumulate offsetting negative energy. Their psyches, or souls, go straight to the primary source without even a tunnel to transverse."

Joe said this with such conviction, no one seemed interested in challenging of how he could be so certain. He continued.

"Yes, Reverend Paul Miller, President of the Southern Baptist Convention, your question?"

"Dr. Cleary, if I am wrong please correct me, but I have the distinct impression that what you are saying essentially negates the need for organized religion on earth. That no matter what we preach, our destiny is already ordained. We die and we make it all the way down the tunnel or we don't. Cut and dry. Have I missed something?"

Joe smiled tolerantly and good naturally without any hint of condensation. "Reverend Miller, you have explained very well why I warned that I did not want this to be a session on religion.

"What I have reported has absolutely nothing directly to do with organized religions. Let me *go out on a limb*. It is my personal belief, not related to Project Omega, that organized religions' most valuable contribution is to provide guidelines and standards for human conduct and interactions on earth rather than preparing them for the hereafter. I hasten to add that a moral, positive life seems to add to the positive strengthening of the psyche's energy.

"Religions have generally been a civilizing force, providing order where chaos reigned, and comfort when disasters struck. No religion has a monopoly on the soul. Does that answer your question, Reverend Miller?"

"I don't know whether you answered it or not. I think you said religions have some useful purpose, but it was a little vague what exactly that is. If we are not teaching the right path to Heaven, then we have much work to do."

Joe laughed, "I'm sorry if I have confused everybody. It is really very simple. Religions can enhance the strength of the psyche, the soul, by encouraging energy-enhancing human activity, and discouraging energy reducing contact - good guy versus the bad guy. The psyche wants to reach the Eternal Tunnel with a strong positive energy force. That is where organized religions can help. That help any, Reverend Miller?"

"I believe so, but like others have said, I will have to give more thought to the meaning.

"While I have the floor, Doctor, would you elaborate on your team's stated quest to discover whether there is such a thing as eternity? We glibly talk eternity in our churches as if it were a given thing, when we really must rely upon Scriptures and our faith as to belief in eternity. Did you, Doctor, discover eternity?"

"Let me correct one assumption you made, Reverend Miller. One of our team's objectives was to determine if the psyche survived the death phenomenon, and if so, was it a singular moment or was it to survive for some undeterminable amount of time. This was a little bit of a stretch of our medical research goal, but we rationalized that our patients would be more willing to subject themselves to extreme hypothermia if they knew what might happen if they could not be resuscitated. Oblivion is not a future sought by many people.

"As for discovering eternity, that is certainly a more complex question. I cannot answer that definitively because my mind is slightly muzzled from a full understanding of the meaning of eternity, which we earthlings have always interpreted as meaning forever.

"What I sense is somewhat at odds with our common understanding. For example, we humans tend to think of time as linear, that is, a straight line from A to B. Yet, have you noticed that our universe is nonlinear? The earth is round, as are the planets. No one has seen a square or flat planet. In my new awakening, I sense that eternity is circular. There is no beginning nor end, nor is it static in size. Beyond that, I have no knowledge. That is as close as I can come to answering your question, Reverend Miller.

"I must move on as others are waiting. I believe I saw your hand raised Rabbi Schwartz. You have a question?"

"Yes, I do. I have no concern, Dr. Cleary, whether the Ten Commandments were handed down on stone, aluminum, or even plastic, nor do I have concern on what we believe to be Heaven and Hell, but what I am concerned about is that you so casually dismiss over four thousand years of Jewish history.

"I need more proof of what you say than just the recollections of a hypnotized and euthanized individual who may be blessed with a vivid imagination."

Joe was quick to respond. "Believe me Rabbi, I do not intend to be flippant nor disrespectful, but there is only one way that I can prove to you, and I'm sure some others, of the veracity of my report, and that is to have a volunteer accompany me into the afterlife on my next experiment, as did Pamela Parker. She is a believer."

That brought a few smiles.

"On the other hand, Rabbi, you have accepted the word of men who have lived thousands of years ago and whose identity is not proven. Even their existence is not proven, yet their words are the basis of your beliefs.

"The same is true of Christians. Your beliefs and all other religious beliefs have a foundation of faith. I do not challenge that for one minute. I am making no challenges, just reporting facts as best I know them. You can, of course, accept or reject them. I have at least provided you with the truth of verified facts to substantiate my report. No faith is involved to believe them."

With anger in his voice, Rabbi Schwartz questioned, "How dare you, Sir, question the word of God? Yes, we have faith, but it is in God whose words have been faithfully reported through the ages by wise men.

"I cannot in good faith tolerate this desecration of the Torah." With that, Rabbi Schwartz rose from his chair and with dignity walked out of the room. There was shocked silence.

A moment later, His Eminence, Archbishop Pietro Allegro rose from his chair, and with a shrug of the shoulders and arms, also left the room. He was followed by the remaining clerics, two and three at a time, although some reluctantly, until the only remaining person in the audience was the atheist, Janet Ogle.

Joe just stood at the podium and watched, not exhibiting any sign of distress or concern. Fred Johnson was fidgeting and looked embarrassed. The Chancellor had left the meeting after he gave his welcome, as did Dr. Stanton, so that the only remaining people on the stage were members of the Project Omega Team. They looked either agitated or embarrassed for Joe.

After the last cleric departed, Joe looked disappointed and even hurt. He later told Frank Picariello that he had at least thought the Reverends Peters and DeHaven had accepted his story. He was very disappointed that Archbishop Allegro had departed because Joe also had the impression the good padre believed his story.

Janet Ogle was looking at Joe with a sympathetic eye. Joe looked down at her, smiled, and said, "Well, Ms. Ogle, you certainly have made your point. There is no God in the audience, or perhaps more accurately, no representative of God in the audience."

Ogle replied, "I know, Dr. Cleary, that you are trying to make light of an embarrassing incident. How does that affect your report? Is God also out of your dream?"

"Nothing has changed, Ms. Ogle, and God was never in my dream since I was not dreaming. Facts cannot be changed by denial. Truth is ultimately stronger than faith.

Chapter 26

No matter how blasé Joe Cleary tried to act, he was deeply offended by the walkout of the clergy. He tried to maintain an *above it all* attitude, but his closest friends, Vicki, Frank and Rosie, knew him well enough that they saw through the veneer and knew he was deeply disturbed.

Fred Johnson was getting ready for the onslaught of the news media once they picked up on the walkout, and he had no doubt they would soon learn of it.

Joe felt that he had failed at the one thing he knew would throw the research into a conundrum, and that was the introduction of religion into the research. He was now sorry that he had agreed to meet with the clerics.

Vicki tried to comfort him that night, and she succeeded to a point, but Joe kept coming back to the project and the reactions of the press and the religious community.

Joe was right. It was not long before the headlines were making exaggerated proclamations: *Church Leaders Reject Research Into The Hereafter; Baptist Minister Calls Death Research a Heresy; Leading Atheist Says Research Doctor Living in a Dreamworld.* So the news media again resorted to the spectacular instead of the facts.

Joe stayed in his home for days, not answering calls. Vicki was the only one he saw, and that was because she stayed with him, afraid to leave him alone in his depressed mood.

In the early morning of the fifth day after the disastrous meeting with the clerics, Joe came down the stairs whistling and smiling, a one-hundred and eighty degree turn in mood. Vicki had arisen earlier and was fixing breakfast. She was stunned at the sudden change in Joe.

"Well, Mr. *Whistler*, what has gotten into you that you are so jubilant this morning after being such a sour puss for days?"

"And a good morning to you, too," Joe laughed. "Can't a guy whistle while he works?"

"Oh, so now you are working, and just what work is that, Happy Boy?"

Before he answered, he grabbed Vicki around the waist, pulled her towards him and gave her a prolonged kiss that almost ended the breakfast effort.

Vicki finally broke away, laughing, and saying, "Whoa there, Mister, if you want breakfast you better lay off that heavy breathing and passionate kisses. Now tell me truthfully, what has changed your mood?"

"You mean I do not even get an 'I love you' before you interrogate me?"

"You can have all the loving you want, but only after you tell me what is going on. I am filled with curiosity that dampens my romantic impulses," Vicki kidded.

"All right, you win, my love. I am high on the excitement of knowing what I have to do to get acceptance of our Project's results."

"You think it is important to get acceptance?" Vicki asked. "By whom? The team members are all believers. So are the Chancellor and the faculty. I believe you. So who else matters?"

"Vicki, I will never convince everyone in the world, and that isn't even my objective. I want enough of the general public to accept our team's report because it will greatly enhance their lives for them to know for certain that life does not end with death of the body."

"Darling, most people already believe that through the teachings of their churches and synagogues. What more will your report add to their belief?"

"Facts instead of blind faith. Even the most devout have questions in their minds at times whether their faith in the hereafter is true. I want to tell them it is true and let them hear the proof. Don't forget the advancements we have made in hypothermia anesthetic."

"OK, so what does that mean? Are you going to launch a publicity campaign, travel the world with your story, write a book, make a movie or TV series or all of the above?"

Joe laughed and said, "None of the above. I am going back into the hereafter and bring back proof that even our resident atheist, Janet Ogle, will believe!"

There was a moment of light headiness that made Vicki believe she was about to faint, but she overcame it. She argued, cajoled, threatened, and used every female weapon she could muster, but Joe was adamant and insisted it was the only way to validate the team's efforts.

Joe made the case that the press and clerics were not impressed or moved by Al Settleman's series of verification tests, even though they proved Joe was really out of his body and observing the procedure in the operating room. Grandma Willett made little impression.

Joe told Vicki, "It is almost like the biblical story of the *Doubting Thomas*, who wanted to put his fingers in the wounds of the risen Christ before he believed. We now have multiple Doubting Thomas's."

Project Omega's team members were no more pleased than Vicki to receive Joe's decision. Rosie Willett and Frank

Picariello flat-out said, "No," to the idea. Joe threatened to get others to replace them if necessary. There was Irish, Italian and Jewish anger spewing forth until Joe finally wore them down by a small compromise. He again agreed to spend no more than thirty minutes out-of-body before resuscitation began rather than the hour he originally proposed.

One of the arguments Frank was making against another experiment was the absence of any clear objective. He did not buy the idea that Joe was somehow going to acquire irrefutable evidence of his journey. Joe did not help his argument by telling Frank he was not certain what he would find as proof, but that he knew within his mind that he would. He said it was one of those newly acquired instincts and knowledge resulting from previous excursions into the land beyond.

The problem was that none of the other team members was blessed with the newfound intellectual prowess from the gods or wherever Joe had gotten his. The team was stuck with their human frailties of not knowing the beyond, although all of them clearly understood permanent death. It was a daily occurrence in the hospital. They feared for Joe.

Chapter 27

The news that Joe and his team were going to try another test into the unknown reached the ears of the Chancellor. He summoned Joe and Frank to his office.

When both doctors were ushered into the Chancellor's office, he said without any other greeting, "I warned you Doctors that you were playing with dynamite by informing the press and briefing the clergy. It has raised a real storm, not only with the public, but now I am getting it from the Alumni Association.

"We depend upon the Alumni for large financial contributions every year. As one Alumnus said, 'I'm not giving good money for some kooky professor to explore a dream world.'

"That was just one call. We have had at least fifty more similar in tone. I hate to do this, Joe and Frank, but as of start of business tomorrow, your Project is finished."

Both Joe and Frank recognized it would be useless to argue with the Chancellor. They knew from experience he was not a *shoot from the hip* kind of administrator and had given this decision careful thought. He had to weigh what he perceived as the value of the research against his continuing need to raise funds for the University's survival. Being a private school, he could not rely upon any government bailouts.

Joe and Frank left the Chancellor's office about fifteen minutes after they entered. Neither said a thing until they were out of the building.

Frank was the first to speak. "Don't take it hard, Joe. We have been very successful, and the team thought your last trip was supposed to be the last. We really aren't losing anything by not doing the last trial."

Joe stopped and looked at Frank with a steady eye like a teacher talking to a reluctant student.

"My dear friend, you are wrong. We did not complete the project because we did not gather scientific evidence that eternity exists. We did prove that people can be resuscitated after a period of death if under controlled circumstances. We already knew that before the tests began.

"You, Rosie and most of the team believe me when I describe *the light at the end of the tunnel*, but I know there is a lingering doubt in the back of a few minds.

"The fact remains the Project has not fully completed its objectives. We need to do this last trip."

"Joe, be realistic, the Chancellor cut off the program. You can't go against him without severe repercussions, and since you cannot do the test alone, you would involve the whole team in the conspiracy and its consequences."

"I am aware of that, Frank, but the Chancellor clearly stated the Project would terminate tomorrow morning. We will perform the last test tonight.

* * * * * *

When Dr. Joseph Raymond Cleary told the team what had transpired in the Chancellor's office, and as a result was planning to do the final test that night, there was grumbling. He promised this Project Omega test would be unequivocally the last experiment.

A very reluctant team began the preparations to beat the deadline. It was a cold November evening, six weeks after the ill-fated meetings with the religious leaders, the one heretic, and the Chancellor.

It was a grim group. No wisecracking by Frank Picariello, the team's comedian. Mostly resigned looks, with Vicki Wentworth trying very hard to control her emotions. She was a nervous wreck. The only relaxed member of the team was Joe, who was smiling, reassuring everyone and promising that by the end of the test, they would have achieved their ultimate goal, the proof of eternity and that human life does not end at mortal death, but continues in another form for eternity, just like most of the great religions of the world had been preaching for an eon. Now, however, the team will have produced scientific proof.

Frank, in a futile but persistent attempt to sway Joe asked, "We all know, Joe, that we have already proved the medical definition of death needs to be revised as a result of our Project, but how has this really contributed to the practice of medicine? Is it really worth the risk to try to convince a few reluctant clerics or one misguided atheist?"

"I'm a little surprised at you, Frank," Joe responded. "You know as well as any of us that the mere fact we will have forced a new look at the definition of death means that some number of people will live because their doctors did not give up just because their patient's heart stopped, their brain goes flatline, or all body functions seemed to have shut down.

"Our report may well stimulate further research and development into equipment that will routinely be used during the treatment of some patients, like our *Refrigerated and*

Warming Dewar. That may permit surgery that would have been otherwise high risk, like the case of Pamela Parker.

"We are on the threshold of understanding the human makeup in terms never before thought possible. We have proved beyond the proverbial *reasonable doubt* that human life is more than the human physical body. We have made faith a fact, and that will revolutionize the human race forever."

"I guess we all understand most of what you are saying, Joe, but I am not clear on whether confirming some biblical beliefs is worth the risk of your life," Frank responded.

"Frank, my dear friend, and Rosie, Vicki, all of you, believe me, I do not have a death wish. I ask all of you to think ahead. Sure, we have established some basic truths about death, but what about the future of Homo Erectus? Is it possible that someday we will be able to control our psyches independent of our bodies? Is it possible that our bodies are but vessels for the soul, and that it is possible for the soul to operate independent of the body?

"Consider the evolution of Homo Erectus alone, perhaps one-and-a-half to two million years old. What will happen to this development in the next million years?

"Think of our dreams. We wander in our dreams into wondrous places we have never seen before, have adventures and experiences totally unrelated to our everyday existence, and meet people we have never met in our awakened life.

"Where do these images and experiences come from? Is it possible that our psyche does take journeys while we sleep, and that our psyche is independent of our brain? Is the psyche where thoughts are located, and the brain is merely an operating mechanism to give sound, sight and touch to our thoughts? In contemporary terms, are brains the computer and the psyche the software? Even that is not an original thought.

"Yes, my friends and colleagues, our efforts are worth the risk because all we have to lose is one mortal body, not the soul, and by so doing we may help open a totally new world.

"On the other hand, I have at least one big incentive to continue my mortal existence and to return from my ventures into the hereafter. That incentive is named Vicki. So, I believe we should get on with the project."

* * * * * *

Once the team members began their preparations, they were all strictly professional no matter how they had felt about Joe going back into the imponderable abyss of the hereafter.

Rosie did her hypnosis process on Joe, and he was placed into the RWD device. Everything went smoothly, and Frank called a heart stoppage when Joe's temperature reached 67 degrees Fahrenheit, 19.44 Celsius. His brain flatlined about five degrees lower. At that point, the automatic timer on the electroencephalograph started the countdown for thirty minutes.

As before, everyone on the team in the OR sat tensely as the timer ticked away.

Every time the team had put Joe down in the RWD they had the feeling they were going against their Hippocratic Oath, *Primum non nocere*, "First, do no harm."

Vicki was obviously the most tense. Her eyes above her mask were pin points of worry.

It seemed like hours rather than just thirty minutes, but the ding of the timer brought everyone to full alert.

Frank Picariello gave the order. "Start the heater, Andy. Reset the timer.

"Vicki, standby with the Epinephrine and Bill, have the paddles ready just in case."

Joe's body temperature began to rise at a satisfactory rate as in past procedures. The crew was feeling a little less tense, but they knew they were approaching the critical phase, the heart beat.

Frank called out, "I've got a heart beat. Temperature is 87, beat at 60 and rising. Still flat line. No problem."

By the time Joe's temperature reached a normal 98.6 and his brain was still flatlined, Frank began to worry.

"O.K. Andy, turn on the pump and let's give his system a little booster." Turning to Bill Ryder, the team's surgeon, Frank said, "Bill, be prepared to give some electrical stimulus through the diodes on the headpiece. Joe may need a little help getting back.

"Rosie, continue your recall commands. Maybe it's noisy where he is and he didn't hear you."

Frank's attempt at levity fell flat. The whole team was working expertly as they had before. They did not need instructions, but it helped Frank's nerves to be actively doing something if only giving orders.

Joe' body temperature and functions except for the brain wave had been continuing normally for fifteen minutes, but the flatline did not waiver.

"Don't anyone panic," Frank said. "Joe said himself that he might be a little slow returning this time but to follow our well-established protocol. Remember, he wanted an hour instead of just thirty minutes. We'll keep him on the pump until we start to get some blips. In the meantime, let's go about our business as prescribed. That probably means more anxious waiting."

Frank could see above his mask that Vicki Wentworth was reaching the end of her self-control. He knew he would have to get her out of the room rather soon or she would breakdown in front of everyone, and that is not helpful in a critical situation.

Thirty minutes had passed, and Frank started reviewing the protocols for the test approved by Joe. It stated that he should be kept on the pump for no longer than two hours. If by then, he had not returned to the world of the living, Frank was to *pull the plug* on the heart-lung machine because any longer may cause irreversible damage to the brain.

After one hour and still no blip, Frank said, "All right, I want everyone out of here to the lounge except Andy Gorham, Rosie Willett and myself. There is nothing the rest of you can do for the next hour. Joe said he would be taking longer on this trip, so let's not jump to conclusions yet. Relax in the lounge, and I will call you if there is any change."

Vicki protested, saying she wanted to stay. Rosie shook her head *no* to Frank without Vicki noticing. Rosie's professional eye also saw that Vicki was on the verge of collapse.

"I can appreciate your concern, Vicki," Frank said tenderly, "but we must follow protocol and not permit personal feelings to dictate our actions. Joe wanted it that way. OK?"

Vicki reluctantly went to the staff lounge with the others. The team took turns staying with Joe.

The next hour seemed to speed by as if time had been reset for a faster pace. When the two-hour alert went off, and nothing had changed with Joe, even Frank was showing the strain.

Frank was thinking, *It was almost seven months ago that Project Omega was hatched by Joe, right in this lounge.*

Frank spoke to the other team members in the OR with him. "I know the protocol says we pull the plug now, but I will take it upon myself as the Team Leader to make a slight change. We will give it another hour. Is that a problem with you, Andy, and your equipment?"

"No, Dr. Picariello, I've run patients longer and they turned out O.K. Remember the Pamela Parker case. I would not advise beyond three hours."

Frank turned to Dr. Rosie Willett. "Rosie, would you tell the other team members we are going for three? Try to look confident, I suspect they are in a funk about now."

"Sure, Frank, but I will probably have to give Vicki a sedative."

* * * * * *

I have been *telling this tale* for the past couple hours straight as it happens without injecting any *inside the brain* details of the players in this melodrama. Now, things were coming to a head, and none of the team was thinking rationally. That is the problem when a research project becomes too personal.

A research team that consisted of a woman in love with the subject of the research, the subject's best friend and second best friend, as well as colleagues that he had worked with for years, created an emotional time bomb.

Watching the time tick away, minute-by-minute, sweat began to form around Frank Picariello's loose shirt collar. All the team members had removed their masks in the lounge, but the three still in with Joe stayed in their scrubs and masks.

At the end of three hours, Frank turned to Andy Gorham, the pump technician, and with choked words said, "Pull the plug, Andy."

Frank immediately pulled off his mask and rushed from the room with an audible sob. He went into the hallway and not the lounge. Rosie followed him out, put her arm around him, but said nothing. There was nothing to say. Joe was gone.

The team members in the lounge heard the commotion and looked through the window in the door into the OR. They saw Frank rush out followed by Rosie.

Vicki slumped in a faint and was carried to the couch. The others were in a state of shock. Joe was not only gone, but the project failed to provide the missing link to convince a skeptical press and public.

Dr. Bill Ryder was the calmest head on the team at that point, so he took it upon himself to follow the remaining team protocol. He called Dr. Arthur Demothenes, a Pathologist who was the University's Mortician as well as a teacher. Doctor Demothenes was also responsible for preserving donated cadavers used by the Medical School. Joe was not destined for that end. Bill Ryder asked him to pick up Joe's body and to put it into the body refrigerator in the morgue as previously planned in the team's protocol.

When Andy Gorham stopped the heart-lung machine, he started the cooling process of the *Refrigerated and Warming Dewar* to reduce Joe's body temperature to delay the decaying process.

Rosie volunteered to take Vicki home with her and keep a practiced eye on her. Vicki was an emotional wreck.

The other glum looking team members attempted to be busy, cleaning up, although there wasn't much to clean, and they all avoided looking at Joe in the sarcophagus-like operating table. One by one they went by the still figure of Joe and silently mouthed a *goodbye*, and left the room with tears in their eyes.

Joe was on his way to eternity.

Chapter 28

Joe had insisted the team's Protocol, their detailed instructions for conducting their experiments, include orders to the morgue to keep his body at low temperatures for not less than three days. His reasoning was that he was not certain whether the in-between world of the vortex-shaped tunnel was a timed transition in a place where time did not exist. He reasoned that a psyche could not indefinitely survive in that state and then return to the body, but still not certain of how long it could remain in a limbo.

Without any particular rationale, the team, including Joe, settled on the three days after which he would be cremated as called for in his trust and will. Frank was the named Executor.

It was three o'clock in the morning on the third day after Joe's passing that Frank was jangled out of his sleep by the ring of his telephone. In his half-stupor of sleep he thought, *another auto accident, I'll bet, and some badly smashed bodies need repair.* Frank was used to those kind of calls, and he was on call that night, first time since Project Omega had started.

Frank's wife, Angelina, lay next to him and merely grunted when the phone began to ring. She was also used to middle-of-the-night calls. She often said, "It goes with the territory. You marry a Doc, that is what you get."

Frank looked blearily at the clock on the nightstand, let out a moan and finally picked up the phone.

"Dr. Picariello," Frank answered.

"Sorry to call you at this hour, Doctor. This is Peter Feaster at the University morgue."

With that information, Frank was rushed into full awareness, adrenalin pouring through his veins.

"Oh, yes, Peter, what's up?"

"Well, you may think I have been drinking or something, I haven't, but about thirty minutes ago I heard some scratching like noises coming from the lockers. Scared the hell out of me.

"I located the source of the noise, but when I got to the locker, the scratching stopped. It was Locker 75, that's Dr. Cleary.

"I can tell you that it took all my will power, but I opened it up and pulled out the rack with Dr. Cleary's cadaver and took a look. He looked quite dead, but had not developed that death hue, grayish color. He almost had a little color in his cheeks, but I checked his pulse and of course there was none, and his skin was the usual cold-of-the-dead in the refrigerated bin.

"So I pushed the rack back into the locker and began to close the steel door, and then is when I saw it."

"Saw what, Peter?" Frank asked.

"Doc, you better come down here. I don't know what is going on, but it seems damn spooky to me. I have been at this business for twenty-one years and I have not seen anything like it. You better come down."

"I'll be there in twenty minutes. Have you called anyone else?"

"No, your the one whose name is first on the call list."

"OK, and I believe Dr. Rosamond Willett is the second name.

"Please call her, Peter, and ask her to meet me there as soon as possible. Do not explain to her what happened. I would rather tell her myself. We should arrive about the same time."

"I'll do that Doc, and thanks."

* * * * * *

Frank made it to the morgue first, but he had not been there more than two minutes when Rosie came rushing in wondering what was happening, and half-scared to find out.

Frank spoke first. "I'm glad Peter was able to get ahold of you. Something strange seems to be going on and we need to investigate."

Rosie asked, "Is this about Joe?"

"Yes, but not about him returning." Then Frank asked Peter to tell Rosie what he had heard and seen, which he did.

Rosie said, "We need to look now, Frank. Maybe he is trying to come back."

"Don't get your hopes up, Rosie. It wasn't Joe's corpse that caught Peter's attention. Let's look together at what startled Peter."

The Mortician led them to Locker 75. He unlocked it, opened the steel door, then stood back, motioning with his hand for Frank and Rosie to look.

On the back of the steel door, deeply etched in Joe's distinctive cursored hand were two words, *Plus Ultra, There is a beyond*, the words of the Spanish National Motto. Joe had not only found eternity, he sent back the proof.

* * * * * *

Joe had made explicit plans for his funeral, which he had passed on to Frank, his Executor, several years before.

Both he and Frank were Roman Catholics, and had attended Saints Peter and Paul elementary school and church. In his will, Joe asked that a funeral mass be held at their childhood church. Eighty-seven year old Father Dennis L. McCaddon, their former pastor, came out of retirement to offer the mass and homily. These are Father McCaddon's words:

This morning, if my words should happen to fall upon the ears of Atheists, they will be as sounding brass and tinkling cymbal, and no consolation can be given. For only souls of real faith can understand words that will bring consolation and understanding of God's purpose in all things.

I am certain that in this church this morning, we all have the same question to ask God. How come? Why? Why Doctor Joseph Raymond Cleary, a man so gifted, so talented, so useful, so kind, so beneficial to society? A man in the prime of life, after so many years of study and labor, but who could give a true service for suffering mankind. Why? So why Doctor Cleary? Why didn't God take away from earth some other man, someone less gifted, and we might add, a man useless to society?

Come to think of it, the members of the medical profession should have the answer themselves. For are not doctors and nurses daily witnesses to the beginning of life and its ending? They certainly realize that their medical knowledge can only go so far, and they surely know that eventually death must take over. In the ordinary birth, they see the transformation: pain and tears before joy and laughter of a baby being born into the world. The medical profession does not discriminate between who is best and who is worst. They treat all, even "the least among us" in the words of Christ. There are no men, nor women, that are useless to society, but only to themselves.

There is another profession whose membership discern life, its birth and death. They are the members of the clergy, ministers, priests, Rabbis. Shortly after birth they baptize the child dedicating its soul to God. They, too, see the futility of life, knowing that one day they will be called upon to bury that body. Nor does the clergy see useless souls, only those in need of help to find God.

Perhaps there is this difference between these two professions. The doctor through his special training sees and treats the body and can immediately say when the man is dead. But the clergyman with his special training in religion, at this particular moment at the bedside, sees not the shell of the body, but looks inside and sees a living soul. As in birth, he realizes that here there is another brief struggle, a pain, a suffering: but the following cry of joy and happiness is not seen or heard on this side of life. But the clergyman knows that this cry of separation is given in death just before another birth, the birth of the soul going into eternity, into a life where there is no more death. As his last mortal task of serving his fellow man, Dr. Cleary performed the miracle of telling us from his new home, there is a beyond. We welcome this proof and wish Dr. Joe a very happy journey into the world beyond. Amen.

* * * * * *

At the beginning of this tale, I told you that by the end of the story you would know who I am. You might ask yourself, if you still have not identified me, who else can read the minds and souls of men and women? Who but I, your Teller of Tales, can delve into deepest depth of human emotions? The fact that I can come and go as I please to other worlds and other minds certainly alerted you to my unusual nature.

I can hear some of you saying, *You're Mr. Death!* If that is what you believe, you are wrong. There is no death. There is only a change of life. Change is the only constant.

Still don't know? There is only one existence that I could possibly be, *I am The Gardener who plants the seeds of life and harvests the blossoms of the souls. I am the light at the end of the tunnel.*

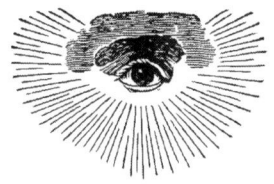

Made in the USA
Lexington, KY
13 September 2012